UNCOVERING ALASKAN SECRETS

ELISABETH REES

LOVE INSPIRED SUSPENSE
INSPIRATIONAL ROMANCE

LOVE INSPIRED® SUSPENSE
INSPIRATIONAL ROMANCE

ISBN-13: 978-1-335-58856-2

Recycling programs
for this product may
not exist in your area.

Uncovering Alaskan Secrets

For questions and comments about the quality of this book, please contact us
at CustomerService@Harlequin.com.

Love Inspired
22 Adelaide St. West, 41st Floor
Toronto, Ontario M5H 4E3, Canada
www.LoveInspired.com

Printed in U.S.A.

I have loved thee with an everlasting love:
therefore with lovingkindness have I drawn thee.
—*Jeremiah* 31:3

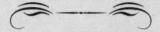

For my son, Lloyd, who always makes me proud.

ONE

"Gimme a break!" Dani Pearce shouted into the frosty air as another ice scraper snapped in her hand, the second one that morning. "I'm way late already."

She threw the broken scraper into the trash next to her porch steps, retrieved a bottle of de-icer from her glove box and sprayed it liberally onto the windshield of her police truck. She'd gotten out of the habit of using the spray due to her daughter's insistence that the smell made her feel queasy. Three-year-old Mia said it was "stinky like a cat's butt," which was exactly the kind of analogy Mia loved to make lately. Everything these days was stinky or poopy or gross, especially boys. And Dani certainly didn't disagree with her on that last point.

"Dani, honey, don't leave for work just yet," her mother, Glenda, called from the front door with Mia perched on her hip. "You have a phone call."

"Who is it?" Dani called back, opening the truck door and activating the wipers. "Can you take a message?"

"He won't leave his number," Glenda answered. "But he said it's important."

Dani checked her watch, sensing that time was slipping away from her. She was meant to be delivering a presentation to her team at the station at nine o'clock regarding the disappearance of a local girl by the name of Jade Franklin. Twelve-year-old Jade disappeared on her way home from school six weeks ago and despite an extensive search spanning many miles around the town of Homer, Alaska, no trace had been found. She'd simply vanished into thin air.

Most believed she'd been snatched by a stranger. Dani didn't agree. She suspected the parents of hiding something. She hadn't made it all the way to the position of Homer's chief of police without developing a strong gut instinct, and her gut was telling her that something was off about the Franklins' story.

"I'll be right there, Mom," she said, realizing that this call might be a tip. "And put Mia down on her own two feet or you'll be carrying her everywhere until she's in her teens."

After switching off the engine, Dani threw

her beanie onto the driver's seat and made her way back inside the house, making a silly face at Mia in the hallway to elicit a laugh. Right on cue, the toddler clapped her hands, doing three little jumps in her denim overalls.

Dani took the phone from her mother and cupped it between her ear and shoulder while pulling off her gloves.

"Hello, this is Chief Pearce," she said. "How can I help you?"

"Good morning, Chief," came the reply. "My name is Colin Nelson and I'm a homicide detective from Memphis." He paused. "It's in Tennessee."

"Yes, Detective Nelson," she said a little irritably. "We may be up in the sticks here in Alaska but we know where Memphis is."

"Of course," he said with an awkward laugh. "I'm hoping you might be able to give me some information about a witness that I'm trying to locate. I have reason to believe he's moved from Memphis to Homer. Are you aware of any men in their midforties who've recently settled in or around the area?"

Dani immediately became suspicious. "Why are you calling me at home? How did you get my number?"

"It's on the police database. I looked it up."

"Our personnel records aren't intended for this type of inquiry," she snapped. "There are official procedures for information requests, and they should be made via the clerk at the station."

"I know that." His tone had become guarded, as well. "But due to the sensitive nature of the case, I need to keep it off the record. I'm sure you know how it is."

"No, actually, I don't," she said. "We don't do things off the record here in Homer. We do everything by the book."

"Come on now," he said, changing tack and trying to sound jovial—as if she couldn't hear the strain under the words. "If we did everything by the book, nothing would get solved, am I right? Bending the rules is what catches the bad guys."

"Bending the rules is what causes criminal prosecutions to fall apart," she said flatly. "It actually helps the bad guys walk free."

"It's not like I'm asking you to search his place without a warrant," he said. "I just want to know if he's there."

"Who are you looking for?" She intended to give nothing away but her interest was piqued. "What's his name?"

"That's the thing, Chief—I don't know his

name. He witnessed a serious crime down here in Memphis and could be the key to cracking the case, but he moved away before we got a chance to take a statement. His old landlady thinks he came into some money and relocated to Homer."

"And his landlady doesn't know his name?"

"He uses a lot of aliases," he said. "It's complicated."

"Yeah," she said cynically. "I figured as much."

The detective ignored her sarcasm. "He's a really tall guy with red hair and a Southern accent. You recognize anyone like that who's moved into the area?"

Yes. He was unmistakably describing Simon Walker, a new and fairly reclusive resident of Homer. He'd set up a carpentry business in a log cabin on the hillside just a short distance from her home. Nobody really knew much about him, other than he'd moved to Alaska from the South—Kentucky, or so he'd claimed—after a messy divorce. He was a man of few words but the work he produced was beautiful, and plenty of folks had already ordered bespoke pieces of furniture from him.

"I'm not prepared to discuss the residents of Homer with you," she said. "I have no way of verifying your identity. You could be literally anybody."

"I already explained that I'm a police detective."

"Then use the police procedural channels," she said, growing tired of his persistence. "I'll write up a formal complaint if you call me at home again."

With that, she hung up the phone and placed it back on its base, her mind wandering to the tall and good-looking newcomer who, if her caller was to be believed, might have some vital information about a crime committed down South—and also a penchant for using aliases. But until she could confirm that Detective Nelson was a real cop, the mysterious Mr. Walker's private information must be protected. She decided to drive out to his place after work and ask some questions. He was pretty private about his past, but he'd remember witnessing a crime, surely? Unless Detective Nelson was spinning her a yarn. Dani had learned a very hard lesson about taking people at face value after she'd been burned by the biggest liar in town. To her eternal shame, she'd married a scam artist who was also a bigamist.

Not only was her husband's whole identity false, but he had another wife whom he'd abandoned in Los Angeles, along with their two children. When she'd been informed by an FBI agent one sunny spring morning that Trey was a bigamist and a financial fraudster who was on the Bureau's most wanted list, her world came crashing down. How could she, a respected police officer, have been taken in by a con man? She felt the sharp sting of humiliation even now, three years after her marriage was annulled. The only silver lining to the whole sorry saga was Mia. Her daughter was a gift from God to bring Dani out of the pain that Trey had brought into her life. Mia had never gotten the chance to meet her father and Dani figured that that was for the best. She was better off without him.

"Who was that?" her mother asked, handing her a flask which contained the wonderfully dark and sweet coffee that Glenda often made on these cold days. "You sounded a little snippy there."

"He claimed to be a cop asking for details about Simon Walker, the new carpenter who lives a couple miles west of here. But I'm not handing over any information without checking out his police credentials first."

"Simon's not in any trouble, is he?"

"I don't think so. He might be able to help with an investigation, that's all." Dani side-eyed Glenda as she watched a smile spread across her face. "Why do you care? I can always tell when you're scheming, so what's on your mind?"

"I just happen to think that Simon is a very nice man," her mother said with fake indignation. "I bumped into him at the hardware store a few days ago and he was very polite and well-spoken."

"And?" Dani prompted.

Glenda ran her hand through her gray bob nervously. "Well, he's in the right age bracket for you and he's single and handsome and sweet, not to mention handy around the house."

Dani clutched the flask to her chest, where her padded police coat was zipped up over her uniform.

"Seriously, Mom," she laughed. "You expect me to date a man based on his ability to fix a leaky faucet?"

Her mother shrugged. "Well, these things are important, honey. And it's been long enough for you to grieve your marriage and move forward, don't you think?"

Dani sighed. Just how did a person move forward after discovering that their spouse had lied every single day of their courtship and marriage? After he'd moved to Homer, Trey had joined her church, claimed a Christian faith and made her feel giddy with the compliments he lavished on her. He also earned a good wage by working remotely for an international brokerage firm. Except his name wasn't Trey, he wasn't a Christian and he was embezzling hundreds of thousands of dollars from his employer, most of which he gambled away in online casinos. After being convicted of multiple offences and sentenced to years in prison, he'd gotten into an altercation with another inmate over a pack of cigarettes. Trey, or Michael Green as he was legally known, was stabbed to death in the ensuing fight. Dani never even attended his funeral.

"I can't talk about this now," she said, crouching to kiss her daughter. "I have a presentation to give at the station."

"Is it about the Jade Franklin case?" Glenda followed her to the door. "You still think the parents are hiding something?"

"I *know* the parents are hiding something. It's just a question of getting all my officers on board."

Glenda grimaced. "The Franklins are a well-respected family in Homer. People aren't taking kindly to you casting doubt on their honesty. Be careful, Dani."

"I'm always careful, Mom." She opened the door. "It's gonna get to twenty degrees later, so I'd stay indoors if I were you. Thanks for taking care of Mia. I'll see you later."

Settling into the driver's seat of her truck, Dani pulled the black beanie over her short blond hair and cranked up the heat. It was times like this that she wished she had a dog for company. These bitter February days were when she needed a warm-blooded companion by her side. Simon Walker had a dog if she remembered correctly—a bloodhound by the name of Lola. That's the kind of animal she'd like staring at her from the passenger seat right now.

Carefully navigating the single-track lane between her home and the highway took some skill, due to the black ice that had formed in the potholes. She kept meaning to fill the holes with gravel but finding the time and the money for home maintenance was difficult as a single parent. She smiled, remembering what her mother had said about needing a handyman around the house. Glenda was certainly right, but Dani wasn't about to go trusting another man anytime soon, toolbox or not. She'd want to do a deep dive of research on them first, starting with a birth certificate and ending with a full interview with their family, former neighbors, longtime friends and possibly their elementary school teachers, as well. Why hadn't she been suspicious when Trey said he had no family to speak of? No roots. No friends. No history. She'd taken him at his word, and trusted his story about wanting a fresh start in a quiet northern town, far away from the rat race in Los Angeles, which he claimed had burned him out. It had all seemed so plausible. After all, plenty of people escaped to Alaska to enjoy the relaxed pace of life.

Banging the steering wheel lightly, she muttered to herself, "Stupid. I was stupid."

The wheel jerked sharply in her hand, taking the vehicle into a fence so quickly that she barely had time to apply the brake. She hit a metal post and the hood folded in on itself with a horrible crunch.

"Seriously!" she said in frustration, setting the handbrake and turning off the engine. "Today is not my day."

After sliding from the driver's seat, she bent over to peer beneath the truck, hands on knees, her breath crisp and white in the silent air. There, beneath the vehicle, was a long log, along with a tangle of thick wire, which was now embedded in and around her tires. She'd seen the log from a distance, but knew her truck could easily drive over it. What she hadn't seen was the danger behind it—the wire pulled low and taut between two metal posts, strong and sharp enough to jam her wheels and cause her to veer off course. There was no way her mangled front tires could function now, even if the engine was still functional beneath the crumpled hood. She'd need a tow truck.

"Who'd do this?" she asked herself, pulling her radio from her pocket. "And why?"

A bullet answered her, slamming into the roof of her truck, the noise reverberating around the snowy hills. Instinctively, she dropped to the ground and used her radio to call for help.

"All units, this is Chief Pearce and I'm under attack on Caribou Bluff, on the lane leading to my home." She stopped and let out an involuntary scream as another bullet landed close by—right next to her foot—kicking up stones and dirt and showering her with a spray of dust. "Gunshots fired. Probably a rifle. Location of suspect unknown."

Another bullet. Another kick-up of dirt. Another reflex scream. Judging by the trajectory of this latest bullet, the shooter was on the move, trying to change his angle to get a better shot. And he would soon have a perfect line of fire. She would have to make a run for it while also leading him away from her home.

"We're on our way, Chief," a voice floated from the radio. "Take cover and stay safe."

She recognized the voice as Officer Jordy Blackwater, a member of her small team down at the Homer Police Station. She knew that any of her officers would respond to her request as quickly as possible, but the station was fifteen minutes away, even at full speed. She didn't have that time to waste.

"I gotta get moving, Jordy," she said, crawling to the fence and squeezing through the posts. "I'm making my way to Simon Walker's place. I can't risk leading the shooter to my mom and daughter. Meet me there."

A bullet whizzed by her thigh, far too close for comfort. Whoever was operating this rifle was skilled and taking his time between shots, lining her up in his scope from his hiding place in the distance. Her best defense in this situation was to be unpredictable, to dart and bounce on her toes like a deer being hunted. If the shooter didn't know her next step, he wouldn't know where to aim.

With no other way of protecting herself, she jumped to her feet and ran as quickly and erratically as she dared, dreading the sharp sting of the bullet that would take her down.

Simon Walker heard gunshots echoing around the hillside and shook his head. Since moving to Homer six months ago, he'd come across plenty of sensible hunters in the area, but whoever was operating this weapon sounded like they were reckless and unrelenting. Whatever animal this guy was tracking would be long gone, surely? Why continue to discharge a gun over and over?

Unless he wasn't tracking an animal.

Something stirred in him, an instinct that he hadn't managed to leave behind in Tennessee, no matter how hard he'd tried. He could sense danger like his bloodhound could sniff out a bear trail. Ten years in the police force would do that to a person, not to mention fifteen years in prison. His long stint in the Federal Correctional Institution, Memphis, had sharpened his mind and taught him to always be on his guard.

Laying down his hand planer on the bench, he picked up the rifle that was leaning against a box that contained the rest of his protective gear—a handgun, binoculars, Taser, night vision device, stun grenade and stingers. As a despised cop killer, he knew he would always be hunted and this was his risk management toolbox. If he couldn't escape his pursuers, he would fight back the only way he knew how: with the extensive knowledge gained as a former SWAT team leader. This constant state of alertness was the way he'd lived his life for the last year, ever since being released from prison.

Raising the rifle to shoulder height, Simon inched his way through the door of his workshop, propped open to clear the dust. On the porch of his cabin just a few feet away, his dog, Lola, dozed in the bright morning sun. The hillside was white with frost today, glinting like a million diamonds against a powder blue sky. There was no denying that he'd found the most beautiful and peaceful place to live, and he'd prayed to God many times not to take it from him. Surely he deserved some respite after the hardship he'd endured?

Louder gunshots cracked the air, tearing the peaceful sky apart. Lola stirred and whined and Simon shushed her with a hand command that told her to stay put. Then he made his way to his boundary fence to take a look at the hillside below.

A woman's voice called out in a panic. "Get inside! Take cover!"

He turned sharply toward the sound to see the uniformed Homer police chief come into view around a craggy rock, darting and sprinting like a gazelle being chased by a lion. Every few seconds, a shot would ring out and she would flinch but continue on her path toward his home, breath pumping out clouds of white vapor. Someone was tracking her.

"Hurry," he called, hooking his gun over his shoulder. He vaulted over the fence and ran down the small slope with an outstretched hand. "Let's get into my workshop."

But they didn't make it that far. They'd only gone a few steps before the chief cried out in pain and crumpled to the ground, clutching her left arm. A trickle of blood oozed between the fingers of her gloves and her face contorted into a grimace, her skin losing color with the shock. In a flash, he hauled her off her feet and ran to a narrow inlet between two rocks, before laying her on the ground and unzipping her jacket.

"Let's look at the damage before we do anything else," he said, his natural authority coming to the fore. "We're shielded here, so ignore the gunshots and try to stay calm."

She panted with exertion, clearly exhausted, while teasing her arms through her jacket to assess the wound on her left bicep. A bullet had skimmed the surface of her arm, torn her shirt and taken a tiny chunk out of her flesh. It would leave a scar and most likely create a small dent on the skin, but he was relieved to note that no serious damage had been done.

"It's not too bad," Simon said, taking a clean handkerchief from his pocket and pressing it to the wound. "Just a graze." Then he rubbed her other shoulder, trying to warm her up. "You're shaking. We should get you inside where it's warm. Do you have any idea where the shooter might be?"

Chief Pearce jerked her head toward the hill above them, her gloved hand clutching the handkerchief to her upper arm.

"There's a bluff just above us," she said between pants. "I reckon he's there. He's been tracking me from my place. We're safe for now, so let's wait for my team to provide backup." She pulled out a radio. "I'll give them an update on my position."

Simon didn't much like this plan. His immediate thought was that the shooter had come for him, and Chief Pearce had somehow gotten caught up in the gunfire. She didn't know that he was a hated man in Tennessee, ruthlessly hunted by two men who didn't believe he had been punished enough for murdering their brother in cold blood.

Officer Thomas Peterson had been shot and killed at point-blank range sixteen years ago, and Simon had taken the rap. Except he wasn't a cop killer. He had been framed while working undercover, and there was no way for him to prove his innocence.

After being handed a life sentence without the possibility of parole, he had assumed he would never leave prison alive, but after serving fifteen years, he'd been unexpectedly released. New evidence had come to light, proving that the judge who had presided over his original case had been bribed to deliver the most severe sentence possible. This miscarriage of justice caused the appellate court to overturn the conviction, declaring it a mistrial. He'd been released while the state prosecutors deliberated on whether to seek a new trial.

Simon's lawyer had argued his case passionately, claiming that fifteen years was already enough punishment, and Simon posed no threat, proven by his exemplary prison record. In the end, the state decided to commute Simon's sentence to fifteen years and allow him to remain a free man forever. Simon knew that the biggest reason for his freedom was the justice system wanting to save face, hoping to avoid the embarrassment of bringing the corrupt judge's numerous high-profile trial bribes into the limelight. But still, it was freedom. He'd take it.

And run with it.

Because as thrilled as he was to be free, the slain cop's brothers had been absolutely livid to learn of his release—and they were dead set on revenge. Knowing that the Petersons would never allow him to live peacefully, Simon vanished from Memphis and escaped to Alaska. But had he now been found? Was *he* the intended target of this sniper's bullets rather than the police chief?

From his kneeling position, he placed his rifle on the flat rock above the crevice that shielded them and then used the scope to search the bluff above. There was a lot of tree and shrub cover, but he knew what to look for—a different color green nestled in the foliage, the glint of a lens, a shape that didn't sit right in the natural environment.

"I see you," he whispered, identifying a figure in camouflage, lying flat on his stomach close to the ridge of the bluff. "But I can't tell if I know you."

This person was so heavily obscured that it was impossible to tell whether they were even male or female. But the stillness of the pose, the accuracy of the shots and ability to track an erratically moving target would suggest a level of proficiency that came from disciplined training. The murdered cop's brothers owned a private security business and knew their weaponry well, so this guy could easily be one of them. As Simon searched the surroundings for the other brother, knowing that the two were rarely far apart, he saw sunlight shimmer on the lens of his own scope and knew that it would alert the shooter to his presence. Sure enough, no sooner had he ducked for cover than the shot ricocheted off the rock above him.

"My officers are on the way," Chief Pearce said, holding her radio in her hand. "Stop moving and don't attract any more attention. Stay low and out of sight and wait for my team to arrive."

Simon immediately shook his head. "Not a good plan. You're gifting the shooter the advantage by allowing him to move freely toward you. You should always be on the attack, even when you're outnumbered or outgunned."

"And what makes you such an expert?"

Chief Pearce said, sounding annoyed. "I didn't know that carpentry qualifications included a module in weapons combat. I appreciate your help, Mr. Walker, but I'd like you to stay in your lane. I am in command here."

He suppressed his annoyance, knowing that she had a valid point, based on what she knew of the situation. Why would a carpenter know more than she did about how to handle a hostile combatant? He couldn't tell her that he was a former SWAT officer with expertise in almost every weapon that existed, and the knowledge and skill required to outwit terrorists, kidnappers, hostage takers, rioters, random shooters and, yes, snipers on hillsides. This wasn't only his lane; it was his highway. And Chief Pearce was blocking it with her standard police training that encouraged officers to always wait for backup.

"It's common sense to realize that if we stay here and do nothing, we'll be in trouble," he said, deciding to be bold. "And I'm not planning on dying today, so I'm gonna go ahead and incapacitate this guy as best I can without killing him." He didn't want anyone's death on his conscience, not least because of the attention it would bring his way. "Hopefully."

She grabbed him by the sleeve of his shirt,

her clear blue eyes locking onto his and demanding he acknowledge her.

"If you defy my instructions on this you might find yourself being arrested for obstruction. That's if you don't get yourself shot first."

He studied her for a moment, taking in her pixie haircut, the strands of short blond hair poking out beneath her beanie. Her face was delicate, like a china doll, with a ski-jump nose, smattering of freckles and Cupid's bow mouth. He suspected that she looked way younger than her years. While she was nothing like the rough-and-ready officers he used to rub shoulders with, she was fierce and clearly meant every word of the threat she'd just issued. There was no doubt that she'd make a good SWAT officer.

He really didn't want to get arrested, didn't want any police officers digging into his past, but neither did he want to wait like a sitting duck in that craggy little alcove. He'd simply have to take the risk.

Popping his head over the shelter for a moment, he said, "He's on the move. I see him headed down the slope, coming right for us." He positioned his eye on the scope of his rifle, which still rested on the flat rock above their secluded spot. "I'm taking a shot before he gets close enough to throw a grenade."

"A grenade?" she questioned while he tracked their attacker. "Don't you think you're being overdramatic here?"

"Never underestimate somebody who wants to cause you harm, Chief Pearce," he replied, taking careful aim. "They're usually more prepared than you, not to mention highly motivated and stronger than you think." This was certainly true of most incidents he'd been called to, where he'd sometimes be greeted with military grade weaponry or idealistic young men prepared to die for their righteous cause. "And it looks like this guy ain't stopping until he finishes the job."

"I hear sirens," she said. "My officers are just a minute away. I want him captured alive and your shot might not be as perfect as you think. You're a civilian, not a police officer. I'm asking you to stand down." She raised her gun. "I'll take the shot."

He eyed her semiautomatic, standard-issue pistol. "You've got a range of no more than sixty yards with that gun. My rifle's range is five hundred." He watched the man reach the bottom of the hill and then head for their position. "I'll scare him off."

He fired his weapon, expertly aiming for the ground right by the attacker's feet, causing him to stumble and crash to the rocky ground. The man rolled over for a second or two before leaping to his feet and hightailing it back up the hill, the long barrel of his rifle banging against his side with each step.

"I didn't hit him, and he's now trying to escape," Simon said. "Your officers should be able to find and arrest him if they move quick."

The chief nodded curtly and pulled out her radio to relay the information about the attacker's appearance and path into the hills, directing all officers to locate and arrest him. Simon desperately hoped they wouldn't mess it up, because he wanted with all his heart to go after the guy himself, to unmask him and find out exactly who was the target of his bullets that morning.

Who was the one in mortal danger here? Him or Chief Dani Pearce?

TWO

"While I'm grateful for your assistance, Mr. Walker, I must ask you not to undermine my authority again." Chief Pearce sat on the stool opposite Simon at his kitchen counter, her sleeve rolled up to accommodate the white bandage that had been placed on her upper arm by an attending paramedic. "Unless there's something you're not telling me, you do not have the necessary qualifications to go around making decisions about when and how to shoot at a criminal suspect."

"I didn't think I needed qualifications to stand my ground," he replied. "The Alaskan State Legislature allows me to use force, deadly or otherwise, to defend myself. Nobody is obliged to retreat from an active shooter whose presence poses an imminent threat."

She tilted her head. "Why do you talk like a lawyer—or a cop? Who are you?"

Simon laughed in what he hoped was a casual way. "I'm just a carpenter who reads a lot of books about police procedural work. I guess some of it sank in. It's a hobby of mine."

"Is that so? Is it also a hobby of yours to carry a Ruger Precision rifle with you at all times?"

"You bet. You never know what kind of animal might come at you in this wilderness." His heart was beating like a jackhammer. "It's a great rifle."

"Do you hunt?"

"Not really."

"You're an amazing shot for somebody who doesn't hunt," she said. "That kind of aim usually requires years of training."

"I did a lot of target practice when I was young." He was anxious to change the topic of conversation. "It's a real shame that the shooter managed to escape, huh? Do you have any leads on who he might be?"

"We're working on it. My team is scouring the hillside before it gets dark and that might turn up some clues."

"I sure hope so. That was some scary stuff out there." If he'd been able to get into the hills with Lola in the immediate aftermath, he could've tracked this guy. He could've caught him. "I have every faith that your team will find him in the end."

Dani smiled, but it looked strained. He knew she felt patronized. He hadn't meant to be condescending, but in all honestly, Simon didn't truly think they'd find the guy. He had vanished like morning mist.

She took out a notepad. "I know you've given a statement to Officer Blackwater about what happened today, but I wondered if I could ask you some extra questions."

He felt his whole body stiffen. What did she want to know? Still, it would just make her more suspicious if he tried to avoid her questions. "Fire away."

"Is there any reason why a police detective in Memphis would want to talk to you?"

He forced himself to pick up his mug of coffee and hold it effortlessly, like a man who had nothing to hide.

"Not that I can think of."

She fixed him with a steely gaze, her chin lifted, and his heart skipped a beat. She was clearly an officer who truly believed in the moral values of a police badge and wore it with the same pride that he used to. But some officers abused the badge and hid behind the protection it offered them. One such officer was his former partner, Colin Nelson, the person responsible for framing him. Colin's betrayal shocked him to his core and opened his eyes to police corruption. Now, he struggled to tell the good cops from the bad. Frankly, he preferred to avoid them all.

"I received a call this morning from someone asking if I'd noticed any new local residents matching your description," she said. "The caller claimed to be a police detective searching for a witness to a crime but I refused to give him any information unless he went through official channels. He told me his name was Colin Nelson."

Keeping his heart rate at a normal pace now proved impossible. The name Colin Nelson hurt his ears like nails on a blackboard. Colin had watched from the courtroom's public gallery while Simon pleaded guilty to a crime he didn't commit, forced to accept a plea deal to avoid the death penalty. Colin had smiled as Simon was ordered to serve a life sentence, clearly happy that his former partner would now finally be silenced. Both men knew who was responsible for killing Officer Peterson, but nobody would listen to Simon. There was no doubt that Colin was now afraid of what Simon might say or do since his release, but all he wanted was a quiet life. Stirring up trouble was the last thing on his mind.

"I've never heard of Cory Nelson," he said,

deliberately getting the name wrong. "Did you say he called you at the police station?"

"No, he called me at home, which is bad protocol. I haven't yet had the chance to check on whether he's a serving officer. It could all be a hoax."

"If he's a real police officer, he'll get back in touch, right?" he suggested, hoping that following up on this matter would somehow slip her mind. "Why should you go wasting your time trying to locate a guy who might just be a mischief maker?"

That was certainly a good description for Colin Nelson—but the mischief in this situation could be lethal. Simon was pretty certain that Colin would be passing on any information he discovered about his whereabouts to the Peterson brothers so they could silence him permanently. The only question Simon couldn't answer was how Colin had tracked him to Homer in the first place. Only his lawyer was aware of his location and he had promised absolute secrecy.

This seemed to be a good time for Simon to remind himself that nobody can ever truly be trusted.

"The detective said that the man he's trying to locate uses a lot of aliases," she said. "So he couldn't give me a name."

This was no surprise to Simon. Colin would have no idea of his new name, chosen to escape the stigma and danger attached to the old one.

"Well, I've only ever used one name," he lied. "And I sure don't remember witnessing a crime." He forced his shoulders to drop after noticing they were high and tense. "I'm not the guy he's looking for."

She scribbled on her notepad. "Seems weird though, what with you matching the description so well and being new in town."

He shrugged nonchalantly. "There are three hundred and thirty million people in the United States. We're all bound to have a few thousand doppelgängers out there, don't you think?"

She seemed to ponder this for a few seconds before saying, "I guess you're right. Do you have any links with Memphis?"

"I visited Graceland once," he said. "Does that count?"

She smiled. "Not unless you stole something."

"I wanted to," he joked. "But I couldn't get the gold chandelier under my jacket."

Her laugh took the edge off his anxiety and he watched her put the notepad into her pants pocket, pick up her jacket from the counter and slide off her stool.

"I should go check on the team and see what they've found." She sighed loudly and rubbed at her short blond hair, mussing it up. "Today seems to be a day for mysterious happenings."

He nodded in agreement, now wondering whether the phone call from Colin and the subsequent shooter were connected.

"You'll figure it out, Chief," he said, despite hoping that she wouldn't. "You got this."

Heading for the door, she waved a goodbye. "Call me Dani. After our successful teamwork today, we should be on first-name terms, don't you think?"

"Okay, Dani. It was nice to get to know you."

The door slammed behind her and Simon let his head drop on the smooth, cool counter. Colin Nelson had found him—perhaps not his address but certainly the town where he lived. And that meant the Peterson brothers would soon be scouring this little corner of the world to smoke him out. The shooter taking aim from the bluff earlier today could even have been one of them. He let out a groan, knowing that this would be an incredibly difficult situation to manage. Not only did he have to lie to the police chief but he needed to lie as low as possible, hoping to evade his pursuers until they gave up the hunt.

Dani stood in front of her team of eleven officers in the briefing room of the Homer Police Station. There was a low hum of voices as the officers exchanged ideas on who was behind the attack on their chief. It had knocked the topic of Jade Franklin off the top spot of conversation, and Dani needed to refocus their attention on the missing child.

"Okay, guys, listen up." She perched on the edge of the front desk and knocked hard on the surface three times. "I know you're all eager to talk about what happened yesterday but I want to put the shooting incident on the back burner for an hour or so to refocus on the Jade Franklin case. I've got a presentation on what we know so far but before I start, does anybody have anything new to report?"

Officer Jordy Blackwater was the first to raise his hand, but then again he always was. Young, enthusiastic and with a sensitive nature, he'd taken Jade's disappearance personally. As the police's school liaison officer, Jordy felt a strong sense of guardianship toward the children of Homer.

"Mrs. Franklin recently remembered something that might be pertinent," he said. "The day before Jade disappeared, a black truck had been parked at the curb outside their house for an hour or so. It might be nothing but we should check it out."

"Did she take down the license plate number?" Dani asked.

"No."

"Make and model?"

"She thinks it was a new Ford F-Series with tinted windows. That's all she remembered."

Dani sighed. "Okay. Well, log it in the investigation file and we'll see what we can do with the information, although it's not much to go on."

She couldn't help but feel it was awfully convenient for Sonia Franklin to suddenly recall that a majorly popular brand of truck was parked by her house the day before Jade vanished. It was yet another weak lead the parents had supplied that ate up valuable time. Quite simply, Dani didn't believe a word that Mr. and Mrs. Franklin said, but she knew that her suspicions were unpopular in the station.

Her sergeant was the next to speak. Vernon Hall was quite a bit older than she was, with something of a chip on his shoulder about not getting the top job. Nevertheless, he was a good man and a diligent officer, who always gave every investigation his best effort. She usually gave him a lot of freedom in deciding how to carry out his duties.

"I just don't understand how a girl can vanish like that walking home from school," he said, echoing everybody's thoughts. "Nobody remembers seeing her on the sidewalk and no store CCTV cameras picked her up. I figure that she'd fight and scream if a stranger tried to grab her, right? Someone would see or hear the commotion. It's like she got teleported right from the street outside school. It doesn't make sense."

"It makes sense if it *wasn't* a stranger, Vernon," Dani said sadly. "When kids go missing, the family is often the first place to look for clues. I don't think we've done enough investigation on the Franklins."

Officer Cathy Merrick shook her head. "Not this again," she said. "Nick and Sonia Franklin are good people. Can we please stop casting doubt on them and focus our energies on finding the abductor?"

Dani had expected Cathy's strong reaction. As a mom of four, Cathy was super maternal and a compassionate police officer with a heart of gold. But she sometimes tended to go overboard when it came to giving people the benefit of the doubt, especially parents who cried on cue.

"Do we know if Jade was unhappy at home?" Dani asked, deciding to ignore the criticism. "Did she keep a journal? Was she communicating with anybody online? Did she get along with her parents? These are all really important questions that we haven't been able to fully answer because her parents won't allow us access to her bedroom. That's where we'll find all the clues, and that's why I've applied for a search warrant."

"Is that really necessary?" Cathy said. "Can't we try asking them nicely instead?"

"We've already done that," Dani replied. "And it's gotten us nowhere. The parents just keep stalling and I've run out of patience."

"Nick and Sonia aren't doing it on purpose. Maybe they're scared because you're turning them into suspects." Cathy held her hands in the air as if in a gesture of conciliation. "I know you're the chief here, but I don't agree with the way you're going about this investigation."

"The Franklins are telling the whole town that the police have done almost nothing to find their girl," Jordy chimed in. "They've now crowdfunded their own private detective to try to locate her. The community has really gotten behind them too. There's a lot of sympathy for the family."

Vernon clicked his tongue. "It's not fair to say we haven't done anything. We all busted a gut to find this kid. Most of us worked sixteen-hour shifts searching the mountains in those first few days. If the Franklins wanna crowd-fund their own investigation then that's their business, but the police department is their best hope of getting Jade back safe and well."

Dani closed her eyes momentarily and sent up a prayer that no one could see.

Please, God, let her be safe and well. Bring her home.

As a strong sense of peace washed over her, she gave silent thanks for the shot of strength. In the six weeks since Jade had vanished, her sweet and dimpled face was the last thing on Dani's mind each night.

"I totally agree, Vernon," she said. "*We* are the best people to find Jade, not some private detective who doesn't know anything about Jade, her family or our community. That's why I want a full and thorough investigation of her home life." She pointed to Officer Blackwater. "Jordy, I want you to visit the Franklins with the warrant to search Jade's bedroom. Focus on her computer first and take a look at the sites she's been visiting and any online friends. Also look for journals or notebooks—anyplace where she might've written down her feelings. Kids often hide stuff like this so try to think like a twelve-year-old girl. What kind of secret spots would you choose?"

Cathy stuck up her hand. "Don't you think

we should call the Franklins beforehand and schedule an appointment?"

"I don't want to give them the opportunity to remove anything from Jade's room," Dani replied. "I've heard your concerns on this, Cathy, but my priority is finding Jade. If I hurt the Franklins' feelings in the process, it's a small price to pay."

A ripple went through her team of officers, some gently shaking their heads and looking at the floor, letting her know that there was dissent in the ranks. The Franklins were popular in Homer, even before Jade's disappearance. The couple had recently opened an upmarket restaurant on the long strip of land known as The Homer Spit, and they had documented their progress in regular blogs and videos that had gotten them a strong following.

"Should we also be checking out the new guy who was with you during the shooting, Chief?" Vernon asked. "We don't really know much about him, do we? He could have a criminal history that he's not sharing. His name might not even be Simon Walker for all we know."

Vernon suddenly reddened and fell silent, acutely aware of the memories he was evoking.

"I'm sorry, Chief," he said, looking right at Dani. "I didn't mean to dig up the past."

"It's okay." She took a deep breath. "We all know I was fooled by a con man."

"Not just you," Cathy chimed in. "We all trusted Trey."

Dani managed to muster up a smile of gratitude. It was reassuring to be reminded that others had also been taken in by Trey's silver tongue and impeccable manners. She'd spent far too long trawling her mind for the signs she'd missed. No alarm bells had rung, no red flags were raised, no suspicions were aroused. It had left her unsure whether she'd ever be able to trust again.

Vernon now stood up and crossed his arms. "When you think of how easily Trey lied to us, doesn't it make sense to check out our new resident? A child vanished only a few months after he moved here and he's cagey about his history. Getting information out of him is like getting blood from a stone."

"Simon Walker is entitled to privacy just like everybody else, Sergeant," Dani reminded him. "There's zero evidence to suggest he's connected to Jade's disappearance and he proved himself yesterday when he helped me escape my attacker."

Vernon kept his arms tightly crossed. "I don't like the guy and I don't like the vibes I get from him."

Dani allowed Simon's face to settle on her mind and considered whether Vernon might have a point. Yet the vibes she felt were anything but bad. They were vibes of attraction that took her by surprise, and she very quickly pushed them aside.

"I'll ask Mr. Walker whether he has any information to share on the Jade case, and whether he has an alibi for the time of her disappearance," she said. "But I can't make him a suspect based on your dislike of him, Sergeant."

Vernon shrugged. "All I'm saying is that we should check him out to be on the safe side. What if he had a connection to the shooter yesterday? Have we fully considered that theory?"

"Come on, Sarge," Jordy interjected. "It's pretty obvious that yesterday's shooter was taking potshots at the chief to punish her for casting doubt on the Franklins. I think the guy just wanted to scare her. Trying to connect the incident to Simon Walker is pretty tenuous."

It was then that Dani noticed Cathy timidly raising her hand. She encouraged her subordinate to speak with a quick nod of the head.

"Actually, Chief, I have some information that might be pertinent," Cathy said. "I got a call this morning from a prison officer in Anchorage. I should've told you before the briefing but I decided to wait until afterward because I didn't want to upset you before your presentation."

"What is it, Cathy?"

"We got a phone call this morning from Spring Creek Correctional Center. Freddy Lomax is out on parole."

The room fell silent and Dani stared at Cathy in disbelief. "Lomax is out?"

"Yeah," she replied. "He was released three weeks ago but stopped maintaining contact with his parole officer in Anchorage after just a week outside. There's a warrant out for his arrest for violating his parole."

Dani was finally able to make sense of the attack. Freddy Lomax had sworn to take revenge on her for testifying at his murder trial and sending him to prison for seventeen years. After serving fourteen of those years, he was now apparently deemed safe for release.

"I was told that I'd be contacted if and when Lomax was released from prison," Dani said incredulously. "And the first I hear of it is three weeks after he gets out?"

"I pointed that out to the prison officer who called, and he told me there'd been some kind of mix-up." Cathy made quotation marks in the air with her fingers. "A miscommunication."

"A miscommunication is what happens

when you get the wrong food order at a restaurant," Dani said, angry at the system's failure to safeguard her and her daughter. "Freddy Lomax managed to use his criminal contacts to send threats to me for five years after he first got put inside, and now he's finally out, he's obviously making good on his promise."

Lomax was a career criminal who'd bitten off more than he could chew when getting involved with a gang that made and sold crystal meth in Anchorage. He'd been given instructions to torch a rival gang's headquarters, but he'd gotten the wrong address and set fire to a disused warehouse where two homeless men were taking shelter. The men died. Dani had been a rookie officer at the time, gaining experience in the city, when she'd witnessed Lomax throwing a lighted rag into the doorway and then running away. Despite being off duty at the time, she had given chase but wasn't able to catch him, so she'd trawled through hundreds of mug shots at the station, located his criminal record and subsequently picked him out of a lineup. She was the only eyewitness, and Lomax made sure to let her know that if she testified at his murder trial, she would pay with her life. She testified anyway.

"If Lomax is on the loose, we should install a panic button at your house, Chief," Vernon suggested. "Are you okay? You've gone a little pale."

"I'm fine." She wasn't fine. "We don't know for certain that Lomax is our perp and I don't want this separate issue to derail the reason that I called this briefing. I'm here to give a presentation on the Jade Franklin case and to implement a new strategy for generating leads." She mentally brushed off the shadow of Lomax as best she could, reassuring herself with the knowledge that Mia was safe in day care and not at home. "We can talk about Freddy Lomax later. For now, let's keep our minds focused on Jade."

She motioned to Jordy and pointed to the wall. "Cut the lights, please. I have some slides to present."

As soon as the switch was flipped, Dani allowed her calm mask to briefly fall, screwing her eyes tight, clenching her fists and suppressing the urge to scream into the dark.

In the early morning light, as tiny flurries of snow settled on the ground around him, Simon yanked the wire rope from beneath the tires of Dani's police vehicle, winding it loosely around his gloved hand and studying it carefully. It was a standard type of cable often found in repair garages and industrial warehouses, but this particular cable had been modified, with sharpened nails glued onto the sides to cause maximum damage. After being pulled taut between the fence posts on either side of the track, someone had obscured the cable from view with a log, which was now firmly wedged beneath the truck's front axle. Dani had been fortunate to escape yesterday morning. Someone had gone to an awful lot of trouble to strand her in a quiet spot. His cursory investigation also confirmed that the shooter hadn't been coming for him after all. Dani was definitely the target and Simon had simply gotten caught up in it.

A police truck came into view on the brow of the lane and pulled up just behind the stricken vehicle. Dani and Vernon then exited the truck and he suspected they'd be angry with him for being there.

"This is the site of a police investigation, Mr. Walker," Vernon predictably shouted. "You really shouldn't be here. Despite what you might've seen on TV cop shows, forensic work is a complex business."

"It's okay, I'm wearing gloves and I was very careful." Simon stepped back and gently placed the wire on the ground. "I'm sorry if I interfered. It's just that I was up early, walking my dog, and I noticed this hadn't been examined yet."

"That's because we had an important team meeting to attend first," Vernon said. "Didn't you see the police tape cordoning off the area?"

Of course he did. He'd untied it. "No. I think the wind might've brought it down overnight."

Dani walked to him and steered him away from the truck with a flat palm on his back. "I understand you were trying to help but Sergeant Hall is right. This is police business and you shouldn't be here."

"I'll leave you guys to it," he said, giving a gentle tug on Lola's collar. "I hope your investigation turns up something useful."

Before he could leave, Dani placed a hand on his shoulder and pressed down gently in a gesture that told him to stay put. He felt himself reveling in the physical touch. After a long time on his own, even simple and fleeting contact was enough to provoke an emotional response. He lived without hugs or shoulder slaps or even a regular handshake. His family was still in Memphis and he saw them very infrequently, too concerned they might be followed.

"I'm sorry," he repeated, before she could admonish him again. "I didn't mean to interfere with your investigation."

She took off her beanie and rubbed her pixie crop of blond hair where it had flattened. Her cheeks were flushed from the uphill walk and a sheen of sweat had blossomed on her skin, giving her a dewy sparkle. In that moment, he wanted to hug her, which was the most ridiculous thought in the world. If she knew he'd been convicted of murdering a police officer, she'd be more likely to punch him than allow him to hug her.

"Have you heard about the disappearance of Jade Franklin?" she asked.

"Sure I have," he replied. "Her face is all over town."

"Yeah, we made a lot of posters. My sergeant wanted to know if you had any information that's pertinent to our investigation. Have you seen or heard anything that might help us find her?"

"I wish I had, Dani. I really do, but I don't know a thing about it."

"Can I ask where you were on the day she was abducted? It's a routine question that we're asking all the town's residents. It was the Friday before the Homer Food Festival weekend if that helps jog your memory."

Simon was glad of the prompt. He remembered the day well because it was an occasion when he'd met a lot of the townsfolk.

"I was volunteering at Bayview Park all day,

helping set up the stalls and tents in preparation for the festival."

"So plenty of other volunteers would've seen you there?"

"For sure." Even though he'd done nothing wrong, he was nervous. "You can ask anybody."

"You're not a suspect, Simon," she said reassuringly. "It's standard procedure to ascertain people's whereabouts when a child goes missing."

Simon looked over her shoulder at the burly sergeant, who was examining the damaged fence posts.

"I get the feeling that your sergeant doesn't quite trust me," he said. "He was asking me a lot of questions about my past yesterday, but I'm not what you'd call a sharer."

"Vernon doesn't always have a good bedside manner," she said with a wink that he enjoyed more than he should. "If you want to keep your private life private, that's your business. I know how it feels to be the subject of gossip."

He had no clue what she was talking about, and his confused expression must've told her so.

"I guess you haven't heard my story through the grapevine yet. My marriage ended three and a half years ago when I discovered that my husband was a bigamist and a thief." She spoke coldly, bitterly. "He was sent to prison, where he died in a fight with another inmate."

"I'm so sorry to hear that," he said, knowing all too well how petty disputes between inmates could spiral out of control, especially among the more volatile ones. "Is the attack on you yesterday somehow connected to your ex-husband?"

"No. We have a theory on who might be behind it and we're working on apprehending him. We're hoping he left behind some clues so we can start building a case in the meantime."

"Well, if I can help in any way, please just ask."

"That's a very generous offer but this is police work."

"I'm talking about help with other stuff, like home maintenance or beefing up your security. Being a single mom must be hard. Even though I've heard people say you're doing a great job with your daughter, you could probably use a little help."

She seemed surprised. Then pleased. "Thanks. It's not often that somebody tells me I'm doing a great job as a mom. I appreciate it."

"You're welcome." He reached into his pocket and pulled out a business card. "Call me if there are any chores I can help with."

She took the card with a smile. "Sure. Thank you." Her focus turned to the police tape that fluttered in the breeze from the fence post next to them. "It's strange that our tape got untied by the wind. We'll have to start securing it better, huh?"

"Good idea," he said. "It can get really gusty in these parts."

He started his walk up the lane with Lola at his side, certain that Dani was watching his every step until he'd rounded the bend and was out of sight.

THREE

Simon scrolled through old news articles on his laptop, reading the details of each one. Some headlines were kinder than others. One simply said, "HOMER RESIDENT JAILED FOR FRAUD," while another was far crueler: "LOCAL POLICE OFFICER DUPED BY CON MAN." Most of the articles contained photographs of Dani's wedding, where she appeared happy and carefree, her long blond hair curled into ringlets and the train of her dress gathered around her feet in a puddle of cream silk.

Then he looked carefully at her husband and grimaced. Trey was tall and rangy, standing with a puffed-out chest and a self-satisfied grin on his face. He had positioned himself almost in front of Dani, placing himself center stage, clearly wanting to be the star of the show. The years that Simon had spent in prison had honed his ability to detect ulterior motives. He could read facial expressions, body language, hand gestures and lots more besides. In this photo, most people would see a happy groom posing with his bride. But Simon saw something else—he saw conceit. He also saw dishonesty.

He wondered whether Dani would be irritated by his digging into her past, but since she'd mentioned her disastrous marriage, he'd been interested to know more. He hadn't wanted to admit it but he was also curious to see what type of man she was attracted to. He tried not to be pleased when seeing that tall men seemed to be her preference.

"Stop it, Gabe," he muttered, using his birth name, the one he'd buried beneath his layers of lies. "Ain't gonna happen."

If one thing was certain, he needed to be pushing this police chief away, not drawing her close. Not only was she asking probing questions, but she also wore a uniform. She was part of a network of cops who all looked after their own. He had been a member of that club once and being ostracized from it had been like losing a limb—but he was firmly on the outside now. If she knew the truth, her loyalties would be on the other side. He suddenly imagined her sitting at home trawling the internet in the same way he was, searching for old news articles about him, her mouth falling open in horror as she read the lurid details of his apparent crime.

Before he could talk himself out of it, he tapped his old name into the search bar: Gabriel Smith. The articles that popped up were as painful to read now as they had been fifteen years ago: "POLICE OFFICER SLAIN BY A COLLEAGUE."

"BETRAYAL OF THE BADGE."

"SWAT OFFICER GABRIEL SMITH PLEADS GUILTY TO MURDER."

His case had been splashed across all the news channels and scrutinized in detail on late night radio shows. He was a decorated officer with an unblemished record who'd reneged on his promise to protect and serve. He had gunned down a uniformed cop in cold blood in order to escape with bags of dirty cash. He deserved to hang. The only people who believed in his innocence were close members of his family.

He hated to think about what had happened, but now that he'd opened those doors, his mind wandered to places he usually avoided. Seventeen years ago, he had been recruited from his SWAT team by the FBI to work undercover in Chattanooga, where the Tennessee River was being used as a pathway to funnel vast amounts of illegal weapons, which were then distributed to the surrounding states via secret storage units beneath food trucks. After infiltrating the gang, Gabriel set about proving his expert knowledge in all types of weaponry, thereby making himself indispensable in their ranks. It took a little over ten months to fully gain the trust of one of the most senior members, who then granted Gabriel access to their network of contacts: the corrupt officials and police officers who facilitated unimpeded access for these weapons to cross multiple state lines.

Gabriel's shock and horror at finding his former police partner's name on that list had been impossible to hide and the gang leader became suspicious, immediately video-calling Colin in Memphis and showing him Gabriel's face. He would never forget the words he heard Colin say—the man whom he had treated like a brother back when they'd patrolled together.

"You'll have to kill him."

But the gang leader had a better idea. Why not set up Gabriel instead and humiliate the FBI? The devious plan was designed to cause maximum embarrassment amongst law enforcement agencies and make them think twice about dropping their men into undercover operations again. After ordering his minions to tie Gabriel to a chair, the leader had then made a 911 call to report that a fight between two men had broken out in a downtown apartment. When a lone officer arrived at the scene, the gang master shot him several times with Gabriel's gun. It was a moment Gabriel had relived over and over, and the memory never faded.

Someone then knocked him out, planted half a million dollars in his closet and searched for bus times to Tijuana on his computer. He'd awoken with his gun in his hand to find several officers shouting and pointing their weapons at him and no amount of explaining could dig himself out of the hole.

Gabriel's FBI handler had initially believed his story and promised to support his quest to clear his name but Detective Colin Nelson, whom everyone respected as an honorable officer of thirteen years, had proven to be the final nail in his coffin. Colin gave his superiors a long and detailed statement claiming that Gabriel had previously admitted to taking regular bribes and amassing a small fortune in a foreign account, which he intended to fund his lifestyle with after disappearing to South America.

Colin's assertion that he had been threatened into silence until that point seemed credible enough, especially considering the brutal murder of Officer Peterson. If Colin's dishonest but compelling testimony were aired in a courtroom, Gabriel knew he would have stood no chance. His lawyer persuaded him to take a plea deal in the face of a certain death sentence. Even though it had saved his life, he bitterly regretted his choice during those first long and dark nights in his prison cell. At that point, death had seemed like the better option.

He gave a start as his phone began to buzz on the coffee table in front of him. Feeling caught out and exposed, he quickly closed the tab on his browser and flipped the lid closed on his laptop. When he picked up the cell and saw an unknown number, he hesitated to answer. It was past midnight. This couldn't be a friendly call, especially since he had no friends.

Sliding across the answer button, he said, "Gabe…" He stopped, and held a closed fist to his forehead, chastising himself. "Simon Walker here."

"Simon!" It was Dani and she sounded a little panicked. "You said I could call if I ever needed help."

He sat up straight. "Sure. What's going on?"

"There's an intruder in my yard. I saw him climb over the fence."

"Why don't you call 911?"

"I already did that but the night patrol can't

get here for twenty minutes and you can be here in five. I just need you to stand guard over my daughter while I go arrest this guy."

He was on his feet in an instant, and he grabbed his jacket, his keys and his handgun. "Are your doors and windows locked?"

"Yes."

He headed out the front door. "Do you have a gun with you?"

"I'm the chief of police. Of course I have a gun. As soon as you arrive, I'll be able to go deal with this intruder without leaving my little girl by herself." Her voice cracked, as the strain seemed to get to her. "I need to leave Mia in safe hands just in case something goes wrong with the arrest."

"I'm in my truck," he said, turning the key in the ignition. "Hang tight, Dani. Keep the line open and give me a running commentary."

"I just heard a window pane smash downstairs," she said. "I gotta stop him coming inside."

"I think it's safer to barricade yourself in your daughter's room and wait for me to arrive. There's safety in numbers."

"I am *not* putting Mia in that kind of danger," she said. "She might get hurt."

"Please don't engage this guy alone unless you have to," he pleaded, unsure why he cared so very much. "I'm only a few minutes away. I see the lights of your house."

"He's inside now. I hear him in the kitchen. I have to stop him before he reaches the stairs."

Simon heard the sound of hurried footsteps and muffled cries, the thuds of a tussle. Then a woman's scream rose from the cell's speaker and he floored the gas pedal, bouncing down the dirt track and veering into the field that would take him on a shortcut to Dani's house. Sliding on the thin layer of snow that had settled there during the day, he struggled to maintain full control. In the darkness, the lights of her home were clear and bright upstairs.

"Dani," he called into the phone on his lap. "If you can hear me, I'm almost there. Look out the window and you'll see my truck heading your way."

Within seconds, a figure appeared in the upstairs windowpane and his heart heaved with thanks. However, his relief quickly gave way to stone-cold horror as realization dawned.

It wasn't Dani.

Simon slid to a halt in the field next to Dani's log-and-timber home. Her police vehicle was parked in front of the garage, clearly angled to prevent any cars driving directly to her front door, and he noticed a thin wire strung across the three small steps leading to her porch. The wire had developed a frosty crust, making its position far more noticeable than Dani likely intended, and the bells attached at either side appeared to have been repurposed from a stock of Christmas decorations. It was a crude early-warning system and, in this instance, had apparently proved futile.

Simon vaulted the fence and raced to the back of the house, the moon providing just enough light to prevent him tumbling over a tricycle left on the path. The back door was open, the pane of glass next to it shattered. He entered with his gun raised, kicking the largest of the shards aside.

"Dani!" he yelled, noticing the disarray in the kitchen, where her chairs had been upended and the crockery from the drainboard had been sent smashing to the tiled floor. "It's Simon. Call out to me."

"I told you to get out of my house," she shouted from upstairs. "Just leave us alone."

He hightailed it into the hallway and mounted the stairs two at a time, weapon lowered but still at the ready. Dani was there on the landing, wearing sweatpants and a T-shirt, the white bandage still wound around her upper arm from where the bullet had nicked her. She was standing guard by a bedroom door that was open just enough for him to see a sleeping child under a duvet on a racing car bed. Dani had a gun in her hand, and a small trickle of blood snaked from her temple.

"You're bleeding," he said. "Where's the intruder? Where'd he go?"

She looked at him in confusion and it was then that he noticed how unsteady she was on her feet. The blood indicated a head injury. Did she have a concussion? Or had she been drugged? She seemed unable to properly focus or speak without slurring. That meant something else was at play here.

"Trey," she said, raising her weapon toward him. "I told you to leave us alone. We don't want to see you."

He stared at her for a few seconds, uncertain of what was happening. The barrel of her gun was level with his chest so he crouched down and carefully placed his weapon on the carpet before rising to stand again while holding out his hands, fingers splayed, palms forward.

"I think you might've taken a blow to the head," he said gently. "You're confused and you need to lower your gun while I check you over for injuries."

"What I need," she said, swaying in the doorway. "Is for you to apologize to me for what you did. You ruined my life and you…

you…you are bad." She rubbed her forehead, leaning against the doorframe. "I'll find another father for Mia. A *better* father. I want you out of my house forever."

He inched toward her, hands still outstretched. He'd seen behavior similar to this many years ago after a colleague was shot in the head during a traffic stop. The nonfatal brain injury caused post-traumatic amnesia, a condition characterized by confusion, bizarre behavior and memory loss. Dani's actions suggested the same type of injury.

"I'm not Trey, Dani," he said softly. "My name is Simon Walker and I'm your neighbor. Someone broke into your house and I'm here to make sure that you and Mia are safe. Please lower your gun."

She looked at her weapon as if it were the first time she'd seen it. "This isn't my gun," she said. "It must be yours. Why did you give me this gun?"

She blinked slowly, head wobbling, the crimson blood from her temple starkly contrasting the alabaster white of her skin. The color in her face had drained to a concerning level but her incoherence was more worrying. She needed immediate medical assistance.

"You're right," he said, coaxing her forward. "It's my gun. So let me take it from you."

"If you're not Trey then where did he go?" she asked, ignoring his outstretched hand. "He was here just a minute ago."

"Did you see which way he went?"

She pointed to the ceiling. "I think he's on the roof." She wrinkled her brow. "But I want him to go away. He's not meant to be here."

Simon lifted his ear and concentrated on listening. The sounds he heard were faint but definitely indicated that someone was overhead. The muffled and indistinct scrabbling made it difficult to pinpoint exactly where the intruder was. Was he on the roof or in the loft?

"Did he go through the loft hatch or out the window?" he asked, seeing red and blue police lights bounce off the surrounding walls, letting him know that help was racing their way.

"Um." She touched her forehead and then her chin with two fingers, smearing blood on her skin. "He climbed through the hole in the overhead floor."

He pointed to the ceiling. "Do you mean the loft hatch?"

"Yes, that's what I said."

The police lights became brighter, indicating that a patrol was pulling up outside her home. As he reached to the hatch cord to pull down the steps, he heard the sounds of running feet on the gravel and a male and female officer calling their chief's name. He shouted out a response.

"We're upstairs! The back door is open."

Dani struggled to focus on him. "Is Trey still here?"

"I'll go tell him to leave, okay?" Simon reached out and curled his fingers around her wrist, wanting to disarm her in case she made a terrible mistake in her confusion. "But I'll need my gun, so let me take it and I'll be back in just a minute."

She relinquished the weapon without a fight and he placed it in the waistband of his jeans, picking up his own gun from the floor and stepping on the first rung of the ladder just as Officer Jordy Blackwater came into view on the stairs.

"Chief Pearce has suffered a serious head injury and needs to see a doctor right away," Simon said. "Put her in your car and take her to the hospital. She's confused and incoherent so ignore any orders she gives you." He then addressed the female officer who was a few paces behind Jordy. "Mia is sleeping so you'll need to wrap her up warm and carry her out to the car. Get them both out of here as quick as you can. Use the front door but cut the wire that's tied across the porch steps as you go."

"Hold up," Jordy said as Simon mounted

the ladder and stuck his head through the loft hatch. "Where are you going?"

"I'm checking and securing the house."

Jordy obviously wasn't satisfied with that suggestion. "Oh no you don't. That's police work. Let's switch places."

But Simon didn't give Jordy a chance to change the plan. In a split second, he was gone, pulling his long legs through the hatch and narrowing his eyes in the blackness, listening intently for where the sounds of movement were coming from. Then he saw the small open skylight in the sloped roof, letting in a cold wind. Someone was scrambling across the metal roof, slipping and sliding on the icy surface.

Crawling to the skylight, he raised his head through. There, at the very edge of the roof, was a crouched figure, wearing a hooded sweat suit with a white logo that ran down one leg. He had reached the drainpipe that led to the ground and was attempting to hug it like a child holding on to its mother.

"Stop right there," he yelled, primarily to ensure that the intruder's attention stayed on him rather than Dani and Mia. "If you give yourself up, I won't shoot."

But the guy was gone, shimmying down the pipe, his sneakers squealing on the plastic as he hurried to reach the yard below. There was now no time to lose. Simon had to make sure that Dani and her daughter could make it out of the house safely. He pulled himself through the skylight and darted as fast as he dared across the roof, keeping light on his feet, before dropping to his knees and gripping the cold drainpipe, breathing hard into the frosty air. The perp was now on the ground on the small patio outside the back door, appearing to frantically search the ground for something he'd lost. Flipping over a chair with a frustrated yelp, a gun came into view and the guy made a motion to snatch it up. Meanwhile, Simon began his descent down the pipe, quickly realizing that he was too heavy for the brackets as they popped off the wall. The pipe disconnected in sections and started to fall. It dropped to a right angle before a strong bracket held firm, stopping it abruptly in midair and jolting him off. He tumbled to the ground with no control and landed heavily on his back with a huge groan.

Despite being winded and in pain, he knew he had to act fast. While still lying on the ground, Simon made a grabbing motion toward the hem of the intruder's pants as he was attempting to make a getaway.

"Stay right there," Simon repeated, hearing Dani and Mia being ushered through the front door and the chime of Christmas bells tinkling to the ground. "Give yourself up."

The guy kicked and shook his leg, while also trying to turn and aim his gun. Simon's own gun had skittered across the ground when he fell, but he still had Dani's weapon as a backup. Trying to retrieve it in this position was another matter, and he could only get a good grip on the handle in his waistband by losing his hold on the sweatpants. Suddenly freed, the guy darted down the path alongside the house, kicking the little yellow tricycle aside with a clatter.

Simon aimed Dani's gun. He wouldn't ordinarily shoot a man in the back, but if it protected those in danger, he had no choice.

"I'll open fire if I have to," he yelled. "Don't make me shoot you."

The suspect stopped suddenly and turned, the hood of his sweatshirt pulled low on his forehead and a ski mask obscuring his features. He responded to the threat by raising his own gun, pointing it sideways like he was playing the part of a gangster, desperate to be a menacing presence. But Simon wasn't that easily scared and stood up slowly, never dropping his aim. His stomach hurt and his back ached, but he forced his body to cooperate and appear unhurt.

Both men maintained their standoff for a

few seconds, while Simon listened to car doors slamming and an engine starting up. As soon as he heard the tires roll away on the lane, he knew that Dani and her daughter were safe. With this guy being on foot, he wouldn't be able to pursue. Not wanting to instigate a shoot-out, Simon lowered his weapon first, and the man began to back away, slowly disappearing into the shadows. At that moment, Jordy appeared in the yard, gun at the ready.

"Where's our perp?" he said. "Did you find him?"

Simon peered into the darkness, seeing nothing but empty space.

"Yeah, I found him," he said. "But he's gone. He had a gun on me so I didn't open fire."

"I'll go track him." Jordy ran down the side of the house. "You stay here."

Simon began to scan the yard for his dropped weapon, awaiting the inevitable empty-handed return of Jordy. Dani's attacker most likely knew these mountains like the back of his hand. He wouldn't be found.

Dani sat by the window in her hospital room with Mia on her lap, reading her favorite book about a monkey who couldn't find his mom. Without fail, at the end of the story, when the monkey's mother finally tracked him down,

Mia clapped her hands and gave a little happy wiggle.

"You look better today, honey," Glenda said. "The doctor says you can leave tomorrow. That's great news, right?"

"I feel well enough to leave today," she replied. Six days in the hospital seemed to be more than long enough to her. She turned the page and the next illustration showed the monkey jumping into his mother's arms. She squeezed her daughter tight, finishing the story. "And Marlon the monkey ran to his mommy to hug her tight and never let her go."

Mia clapped her hands, kicking her plump legs in her patterned leggings and furry boots.

"Again, again," she said.

But a knock at the door interrupted their family time and a moment later, Simon popped his head into the room.

"Hi there," he said with a wave. "I got a message that you wanted to see me."

"Yes," Dani said, nerves jangling at the sight of him. "Thanks for coming."

She handed Mia to Glenda, giving the toddler a kiss on the top of her head. "Be a good girl for Nanna, sweetheart, and have fun staying at her house."

"You should come stay with us too," her mother replied. "We'll take care of you both."

"You know I can't do that." Dani refused to even allude to danger when Mia was present so she resorted to using metaphors. "The weeds in my yard could scratch Mia so I need to pull them up. If I move to your house, the weeds might grow there, as well."

Her mother nodded, understanding that Dani would never ever risk leading her attacker to her daughter. She'd have to catch this guy instead.

"Who is that?" Mia asked, pointing to Simon. "He's tall like the sky."

Simon grinned and Dani's heart lifted for the first time in what felt like forever. His smile was warm and soothing, chasing away the shadows that had settled over her. He was unshaven today and his stubble was the color of the terra-cotta pots on her deck—an earthy orange that she loved. She'd never been attracted to redheads previously, preferring dark-haired men like Trey, but red hair suited Simon. *Everything* suited Simon.

He had a noble quality that had thrown her off guard on their very first meeting. His shoulders were always pulled upright and he was careful to be respectful, like an old-fashioned gentleman. When you added his beautiful green eyes and wide, even smile into the mix, he was quite the heartthrob. But there was a part of him that he kept closed off and she didn't like secrets.

"This is Simon," Dani said, moving to stand next to him. "Simon, this is my daughter, Mia, and my mother, Glenda. They've been visiting a lot and keeping me company while I recover."

"Do you have a hamster?" Mia asked him at a sudden rush. "Or a rabbit? Or a monkey?"

"No," Simon replied. "But I have a dog called Lola and her nose is twenty times stronger than your nose."

Mia covered her nose with a flat palm, giggling and wriggling in her grandmother's arms. "It must be ginormous."

Dani laughed. "Ginormous is Mia's new favorite word."

"Her nose isn't big," Simon explained. "It's just really, really smart."

Mia was now transfixed. "Can I see her nose?"

"I left Lola at home today, but you can come visit her," he said with a quick glance at Dani. "If your mom says it's okay."

"We'll see," Dani said, going to open the door. "But right now, you gotta go home and eat dinner." She gave her daughter another kiss and playfully pinched her cheek. "I'll see you tomorrow, sweetheart. I love you."

With a quick wave, they stepped out into the corridor, where Glenda put the toddler on her feet. Mia broke into a skip holding Glenda's hand. Closing the door, Dani offered Simon a chair, but he chose to lean against the windowsill and cross his long legs at the ankles, jeans riding up over his chunky boots at the hem. Yes, this man was definitely as tall as the sky.

"How are you feeling?" he asked. "Nobody would give me any information when I called the police station."

"You called the station to check on me?"

"Of course I did." He said it like it was a no-brainer. "I've been thinking about you every day. You took a really bad blow to the head."

Her color rose and she ran her fingers through her hair, which she hadn't washed since the day before. Why hadn't she put on a little blush? Or styled her hair? She must look terrible in her old sweats and fleecy socks.

Then she got a hold of herself and realized how ridiculous she was being. This man was somebody she knew nothing about, and Vernon's words returned to haunt her: *His name might not even be Simon Walker for all we know.*

"The doctors told me that I suffered a head injury that caused my brain to go haywire," she said, sitting in the chair by her bed. "But fortunately, there's no lasting damage and I can return to work in two weeks' time. It's just so weird that I don't remember a single thing about what happened."

"You remember nothing? Not even how you got the injury?"

She shook her head. "It probably happened in the kitchen. Vernon thinks the guy used my cast-iron skillet as a weapon because he found strands of my hair on the underside. Scuff marks made by sneakers show that we must've tussled on the kitchen floor before one of us chased the other upstairs." She rubbed her temple with two fingers. "I just wish I knew what happened and, more importantly, that I could remember what my attacker looked like."

"It seemed to me that you were standing guard outside Mia's room," he said. "Even with a serious head injury, your first thought was protecting your daughter. You're one fierce momma, you know that?"

She smiled weakly. She sure didn't feel like she deserved any praise. Why hadn't she left her home until the panic alarm could be installed and extra security features put in place? She had been complacent, thinking that she was strong enough to take care of herself. Instead, she'd put her daughter at risk.

"Thanks for the praise and thanks for also returning my gun to Jordy." She looked at the floor, tracing the outline of a tile with her fluffy sock, steeling herself to broach a subject that was kind of embarrassing. "I read your statement about the night I was attacked, so I have a good understanding of what happened after you got there." She took a deep breath. "Apparently I mistook you for Trey."

"You did," he confirmed. "At first anyway. You were really confused."

She crossed her hands in her lap, fidgeting nervously. She suspected that some part of her was still seeking closure on that chapter of her life and her momentarily damaged brain had seized the chance to vent her frustrations on Trey. She often imagined having a final conversation with him, where she would tell him he was a terrible person.

"Do you remember that I told you about my husband, Trey?" she asked Simon tentatively. "The one who forgot to tell me that he was already married?"

"Yeah, I think you mentioned him."

She threw him a wry smile, guessing that he'd searched the internet to find out all the gritty details. After all, she'd have done the same thing.

"I still hold a lot of hurt and anger about what he did to me," she said, rising to stand and folding her arms. "I'm sorry if my anger was misdirected at you. I wasn't in charge of my emotions."

"It's okay," he said, walking across to place a reassuring hand on her shoulder. "You were actually very calm and controlled and you didn't say or do anything that you should be ashamed of."

She let out the breath she'd been holding in. That was a relief.

"And I hope you find a replacement father for your daughter," he continued. "I have no doubt there are plenty of good men who'd happily take the job."

"A replacement father?" She laughed nervously. "What do you mean?"

"You said you wanted to find a new dad for Mia," he explained. "And I think it's a great idea. You both deserve a second chance with a man who treats you way better than Trey ever did."

She sank the heels of her hands into her eyes and groaned. She hadn't seriously considered dating since the annulment of her marriage, but her head injury had obviously betrayed her innermost desire. Clearly, she *did* want someone in her life, and she was mortified to have revealed such personal information to Simon.

"Don't be embarrassed," he said. "I deliberately left that part out of my statement. I figured it wasn't relevant."

"Thank you," she said. "Thank you so much."

"I didn't want you to be inundated with offers," he said, obviously trying to lighten the atmosphere. "If word got out that you were looking for a husband, it might cause gridlock on the highway into Homer."

She laughed and playfully punched his chest. "If you're thinking of applying for the job yourself you should know that you're already a vast improvement on the last one. At least I know your real name."

His face turned immediately stony and he took a step back, blinking quickly as if she'd insulted him.

"Hey, I'm only goofing around," she said, realizing she'd overstepped. "I didn't mean to imply that you're interested in me. I'm sorry—I shouldn't have said anything."

She forced herself to stop babbling and instead allowed an agonizing silence to settle in the room.

"I gotta go," he said after a few humiliating seconds had passed. "I have a cabinet to finish. I'll see you soon."

Without even waiting for her to say goodbye, he rushed through the door and let it slam behind him.

FOUR

Simon loved snow. He'd loved it ever since he was a child growing up in Memphis. Major snowfall in his home city didn't happen very often, so any of the white stuff, even a dusting, caused a whole lot of excitement. Schools would close, the grocery stores would quickly sell out of bread and milk, and kids would congregate in the park opposite his duplex home. Now, looking out his living room window in Homer, he was reminded of those happy childhood days, when he'd fly out the door while his mother chased after him with a hat and scarf. Aside from a huge Memphis snowfall in '94, he'd never seen snow like this before, blanketing the hillside and bluffs in a pure and unblemished layer of white.

From his wide-open spot on the hill, he could see the majestic sweep of Kachemak Bay and its stunning backdrop. The mountains with jagged peaks looked like they had been carved with a knife. His view wasn't as good as the one Dani enjoyed at her place, but it was plenty good enough to settle his weary spirit and calm his mind. He'd researched the town in great detail and chose it not only for its beauty but because it was known as "the end of the road." There was just one road leading in and out of Homer, which meant that anyone coming for him would have just one access route. Those things were important considerations now. By the time he'd been released from prison, he had lost everything—his house, his reputation and his means of supporting himself. His only option had been to go live with his parents while he decided on a new name and new town. But it hadn't taken long for the Peterson brothers to target him there with silent phone calls and the spraying of vile graffiti on and around the house. He couldn't prove it was them, of course, but they would casually walk along the sidewalk each day, ensuring he could see them through the window. They stared with such hatred that when an anonymous gunman shot two bullets into the front door in the middle of the night, he wasn't really surprised. He had scraped together as much cash as he could before fleeing to Homer, anxious to prevent his parents being caught up in retribution that was intended for him.

He hadn't been back to Memphis since leaving and probably never would. He had seen his parents just once in the last six months, meeting them in Vancouver to celebrate Christmas. He didn't feel safe enough just yet to inform his family of his exact whereabouts. It wasn't that he didn't trust them, but they might inadvertently reveal something to the wrong person or absentmindedly post a photograph of their visit on social media. It was best not to take chances.

He'd fallen in love with Homer and was protective of his place there. This was God's amazing creation—right here on his doorstep—and he didn't want to lose it, but the Peterson brothers, with the assistance of Colin, were closing their net. All he could do was hope that they wouldn't discover his address. Literally nobody from his old life knew that information. Even his lawyer only had a PO box address, which he used to send any legal documentation pertaining to Simon's overturned sentence.

Being totally alone was tough. Simon wanted the same things as most other single men at forty-five: a wife, children, a happy family life and a supportive church community. It didn't seem like much to ask, but as far as he could tell, God wasn't quite ready to give him the peace he craved just yet. He accepted it with humility.

The one part of his life that he struggled to deal with was the constant lying, especially to Dani. She deserved so much better from him. The way he'd hightailed it out of her hospital room earlier that day must've hurt her feelings, but she'd gotten too close to the truth and he couldn't bear to look her in the eye. He felt himself growing closer to her with each meeting and whenever she talked about her dishonest husband, he felt physically sick, knowing that he was also feeding her lies.

"What am I gonna do about this, Lola?" he asked his ever-faithful dog, rubbing her ear where she rested her head on his knee. "'Cause my feelings have to go somewhere."

She lifted her head and whined, as if she understood his predicament, and he laughed, scratching beneath her chin. "I guess you're the only girl for me, huh?"

His cell buzzed in his jeans pocket and he jumped. The double danger of being hunted by the Petersons and the threat of Dani's stalker had heightened his senses. He was skittish. Sliding out his phone, he saw a familiar name on the display: Jeff Moore, his attorney in Memphis.

"Hey, Jeff," he said, reminding himself to

be super vigilant and give away no unnecessary information. "This is a surprise. I don't want to offend you, but I hoped I'd never have to talk to you again."

"No offense taken," Jeff replied, a low laugh rumbling through the speaker. "I totally understand where you're coming from. Do you have a few minutes for a chat, Gabriel?"

He balked. "Can you avoid calling me Gabriel? I'm trying to get out of the habit of answering to my old name."

"What else can I call you? I don't know what name you're using now."

"Just call me John."

"All right, John. I'm afraid I'm calling with some worrying news."

He sat up straight. "What happened?"

"Our law offices suffered a break-in a few days ago. Nothing was taken but our client files were accessed."

"You got to be kidding me." Simon stood and began to pace, Lola following at his heel. "You assured me that your systems were watertight in terms of security."

"They're the best that money can buy," Jeff said. "But the software tools used in the hack were incredibly sophisticated. Our IT guy says it was an expert job."

"Whose data did they target?"

"That's what we've been looking into since it happened." Jeff paused. "And today, we discovered that only one client's data was breached."

"Mine."

"Yes. I'm sorry, Gabriel." Jeff quickly corrected himself. "I mean John."

Simon could barely speak due to the effort required to hold in his frustration.

"You are the only person in the world who knows where I live." His teeth were gritted. "Not even my parents have that information. My own mother and father can't visit me at my home because of the security risk. Do you know how much effort it takes to keep that kind of secret from people you love? And now it seems like it was all for nothing."

"Our files only store a PO box address for you in Homer," Jeff said. "And your cell phone number was divided up and stored across two separate locations so they only managed to access the last four digits."

"The PO box address is all they need to come looking for me," Simon argued. "It's enough information for Colin Nelson to call the chief of police here in Homer and ask her if she knows anybody who fits my description."

Jeff fell silent for a few moments.

"Do you want me to involve the FBI?" he

asked. "We could get Nelson arrested if we can link him to the break-in. We have some security footage. It's dark and grainy but the Bureau might be able to clean it up."

"No way do I want the FBI involved," Simon said, raising his voice. "That would only draw attention to me. The whole reason I'm in Alaska is to hide away. There's literally nothing I can do except hope the Petersons fail to find my home and eventually give up trying."

"The sensible option is to get on the move."

This suggestion almost moved Simon to tears. "This town is the first place that's made me feel happy in sixteen years. It's my home now and I'll fight to stay. Besides, there's a woman here who needs me right now."

"A woman?" The surprise in Jeff's voice was clear. "Are you dating? Does she know about your past?"

"I'm not dating anybody," he said defensively. "And if I were, it's my business whether I divulge my history."

"You killed a man. Speaking ethically, I'd say you have an obligation to give full disclosure."

Simon sat down heavily and leaned forward with his elbows on his knees, head hanging in disappointment and sadness.

"I didn't kill Officer Thomas Peterson," he said quietly.

"Listen." That word carried a weight of weary frustration. "Let's quit with the denials, huh? You served your time and you can drop the act. You pleaded guilty and there's nothing to be gained from now pretending to be innocent, especially with me."

"I *am* innocent."

"I deal with murderers all the time and almost every single one of them finds someone else to pin the blame on."

Simon's stomach lurched to be lumped together with the worst of society, the ones who preyed on the weak and vulnerable. That wasn't who he was.

"You're a good attorney, Jeff, but a lousy friend."

"You did something heinous," Jeff replied, clearly irritated by the accusation. "And you were fortunate to get your sentence overturned on a technicality. When the state was considering a re-prosecution, I argued against it based on your admission of guilt and the good work you did in prison to redeem yourself. The mentorship program you set up in the penitentiary has helped hundreds of inmates turn their lives around and earned you a lot of respect from the top brass. I don't get why you claim to be innocent now. What does it accomplish?"

Simon had had enough of this conversation and wanted to get back on track.

"I don't expect you to understand my viewpoint but I *do* expect you to safeguard my personal data. That's the reason you called in the first place, isn't it?"

Jeff now had the good grace to be a little humbler.

"You're absolutely correct," he admitted. "We got caught out by a slick and sophisticated hack that's exposed you to danger. The firm would like to offer you a generous compensation package to assist you in relocating from Homer."

"I told you already—I'm not going anywhere."

"Why don't you think about it? The Peterson brothers are smart. They haven't put a foot wrong since you got out of prison, at least not publicly, but they've made plenty of covert threats against you that we need to take seriously."

"I'll handle this my own way," Simon said. "I'll maintain a low profile."

"It's a small town, John, and small towns don't let you hide so easily. Would you at least agree to making a complaint against Colin Nelson for calling the Homer police chief under false pretenses? That would send a strong message that you're prepared to fight back."

"Absolutely not. That's what he wants. He's waiting for me to show myself."

"There's a lot of bad blood between you two guys, right?" Jeff asked. "You accused Nelson of some pretty bad stuff before you switched to a guilty plea. I wasn't your attorney back then, so I don't have the notes on what happened."

Simon no longer wanted to think about Colin Nelson and his apparent invincibility. But, of course, Colin *was* invincible and he knew it.

"Thank you for letting me know about the security breach," he said. "I'll cancel my PO box address and set up a new one in the next town over. I'll notify you of the new information once it's established."

Jeff sighed. "I'm sorry we caused all these problems for you."

"Why should you be sorry?" Simon said bitterly, Jeff's earlier words having cut him deeply. "If I killed a man, I deserve it, don't I?"

"Whatever you deserve is a matter between you and God. It's not for me to judge."

"Well, that's one thing we can agree on," he said. "Call me if there are any new developments."

Simon hung up the phone, tossed it onto the couch next to him and brought his hands together in prayer. Jeff had reminded him that only one opinion counted and that was the Lord's. Being despised and reviled had brought Simon closer to God and strengthened his faith beyond his wildest imagination. Once he'd gotten over the shock of being incarcerated, he'd set about making a difference to those inmates who also understood how it felt to be cast out of society. He'd found a purpose in life and a way to serve God with a pure heart.

He prayed often as a general rule, but this time he prayed with extra fervor, asking for something that he needed now more than ever—someone who believed in him.

Dani watched Simon's long legs drop through the skylight and come to rest on one of the beams in her loft. She had been sitting there, cross-legged, an old toolbox at the ready, just in case he needed something from it. She felt so useless while he saw to her broken drainpipes, repairing them after they were torn from their fixings during the break-in.

"That's some view you got up there," he said, crouching in the small space with its sloping ceiling. "It's almost worth freezing my butt off."

"Yep, the Kenai Mountains are something else, aren't they? This place belonged to my grandma and I inherited it from her last year. I love it to bits, but the upkeep is hard work." She sucked in air through her teeth. "And expensive."

"I hear you. My folks loaned me the deposit for my place and I'm determined to pay them back but it's tough."

He stopped abruptly, the way he often did when veering onto more personal topics, as if he was worried about saying something he shouldn't. She opened her mouth to ask about his parents, but he jumped into the gap.

"All your pipe-work is now fully repaired," he said. "And I cleaned the muck and leaves from your gutters. That's one less job for you to worry about."

"Thank you." She was truly grateful for anything that made her life easier. "I've been sitting here just in case you needed something from my granddad's old toolbox." Holding up a rusty metal box with a warped lid, she added, "To be perfectly honest with you, some of these tools probably belong in a museum."

He scooted along the beam and crouched next to her. The narrow space smelled mostly of cedar and pine but the discolored loft insulation nestled between the beams had seen better days and a slight note of damp had crept into the fibers.

"It's okay," he said, pointing to his well-stocked tool belt. "I had everything I needed right here."

She smiled. "I guessed you'd arrive with your own tools. My mom was right."

He shot her a quizzical look.

"My mother thinks I need a handyman," she explained. "And you're top of her list."

"Well, she's not wrong. Your insulation needs replacing and your gutters have seen better days. The metal roof is holding up pretty well but the chimney breast could do with some new sealant and one of those skylight window frames is starting to rot." He must've realized how negative he sounded. "But the inside is immaculate and you obviously keep a really nice home."

She laughed, heading down the loft steps to the landing below. "This house will probably crumble to dust around me, but all the while, I'll be plumping the cushions and pretending I don't see the chimney falling down."

"The chimney's not gonna fall down," he said, following behind. "Not yet anyway. I'll seal it up for you and replace the cracked gutters while I'm at it. If you'd like my help, that is."

This was the kindest offer anyone had made

to Dani in a very long time and she swallowed away a strong and unexpected emotional response.

"Some help with the house would mean the world to me," she said. "But I won't be able to pay you."

"I wouldn't take any money even if you wanted me to," he said with a dismissive wave. "We're neighbors, right? We should have each other's backs."

It had been a while since a man had prioritized her safety and well-being, and it gave her a warm and fuzzy feeling. Simon was slowly creeping his way into her affections, but she still didn't know much about him. Who was he? What was his background? What kind of a life had he left behind in Kentucky? His recent divorce seemed like a good place to start probing, but she didn't want to be too blatant about it.

"I bet your wife was sorry to lose your skills around the house," she said lightheartedly.

"My wife?"

"You recently got divorced, right?" She laughed. "Don't tell me you forgot about your ex-wife already."

"Oh right! My wife." He shook his head as if bringing the memories back. "I think she's doing fine."

"Do you stay in touch with her?"

"No. I'd rather leave it all behind, you know?"

Oh boy, did she ever know. Some days she wanted to run from her past as fast as her legs could carry her, but it followed her everywhere, refusing to be forgotten.

"Did you have any kids together?" she asked.

"No."

She waited for him to elaborate, to explain that they'd been unable to conceive or perhaps had decided not to, but he remained resolutely silent. It was then she realized how intrusive she was being, spurred on by her own distrust and suspicion.

"I'm sorry," she said. "I'm kind of nosy when it comes to new people. I find it hard to take them at face value."

"I can understand why. After what you've been through, you don't want to take any chances, right?"

"Right." She had a sudden urge to open up emotionally. "I felt like such an idiot after Trey got arrested. I was too ashamed to show my face for weeks, thinking that everybody was laughing at me. Then after I stopped feeling humiliated, I got angry, and after I stopped being angry, I started to grieve. The grief is actually the hardest part. I wish I could go back to being angry again because at least I didn't cry so much. Sometimes the sadness is overwhelming, like the walls are closing in and I'll never be able to get out."

"Kind of like being in a prison cell?" he suggested.

"Yeah. Do you feel it too?"

"You have no idea how much."

"I guess that you and I aren't so different," she said. "We both have a past that we're trying to leave behind. Is Homer helping you heal your wounds?"

He broke into a wide smile. "It is. I love it here. These mountains feel like freedom to me." The smile slid from his face. "I hope I get to stay."

"Of course you'll get to stay." She punched his shoulder playfully. "Why would you ever need to leave?" She tried to tread carefully. "Is there something you're not telling me, perhaps?"

"Oh it's nothing specific," he said. "It's just that none of us knows what the future holds. Your whole life can change in an instant." His face took on a faraway expression. "I try not to take anything for granted."

She could see his pain clearly now and it drew her in. She took a step forward, reaching out to touch his arm, but thought better of it at the last moment and withdrew.

"Is that what happened with your wife?" she asked. "Did she accuse you of taking her for granted? If you feel responsible for the marriage breakdown, that might be why you're hurting so much."

He looked at her as if she was speaking another language, his brow furrowed and head tilted slightly. She'd either gotten things totally wrong, or he was puzzled as to why she'd intruded on his private life again.

"I did it again, didn't I?" she said, holding her palms in the air. "I'm getting too personal."

"It's okay," he said. "You're a cop. It's second nature."

She didn't want to make excuses, but instead hoped he would understand her reasons.

"I must come off as a snoop," she admitted. "I don't mean to pry, but I just can't help myself." She wrung her hands. "I wish I didn't feel the need to delve into your personal life like this. It's just that I don't know a thing about you."

He gazed at her for what felt like an eternity, searching every inch of her face with his green eyes, which looked to be growing moist. Was he getting upset?

"My birthday is on June ninth," he said. "When I was a kid, I wanted to be a math teacher. I was captain of the school baseball team but I wasn't the best player. My dad is a retired accountant and my mom works in school administration. My folks have been married for forty-seven years. We're a close-knit family but I don't get to see them as often as I'd like. I moved to Homer to live a quiet and peaceful life far away from all my problems." He touched her cheek and her breath caught in her throat. "I know that you need honesty from me, but that's as much as I can give you right now."

She blinked rapidly, the moment having escalated to something far beyond her expectations.

"Thank you," she managed to say, enjoying the warmth of his fingers on her skin. "I don't have any right to know a single thing about you, but you offered up that information willingly and I appreciate it."

"You're welcome." He slid his hand down to her chin and let his index finger rest there for a second or two. "And for the record, I don't think you're a snoop. You're a good cop and a kind person who's been burned by a con artist. You don't ever have to apologize to me for asking questions."

She nodded, her words failing her for a moment.

"And now I'd like to fix some new bolts on

your doors," he said, pulling back his shoulders with a big breath and creating some space between them. "I know you've got new security measures that were put in place by the mayor's office, but you can never be too secure."

"I got three panic buttons installed. They alert all the emergency services in Homer," she said, the familiar sensation of anxiety now returning after a brief respite. "I hope I never need them, but we're no closer to finding the guy so it's better to be prepared."

"You got a good idea who it is though, right?"

"We're pretty sure it's a man that I put away for murder fourteen years ago in Anchorage. He just got out on parole."

"Well, I'll pray that he gets picked up soon enough and you can have your daughter back."

The thought of Mia made Dani want to weep, but she dug her nails into her palms and fought off the tears.

"I just hope that Lomax really is the guy we're after," she said. "All the bad feelings surrounding the Jade Franklin case muddy the water a little. What if my attacker is someone closer to home? There are plenty of people in Homer who don't seem to like me at the moment."

"Your job is to be their police chief, not their friend."

Simon said this so matter-of-factly that she was instantly reminded of the responsibility of her position of authority, her obligation to investigate crimes diligently rather than give people an easy ride.

"How true," she said. "Thank you. I needed to hear that. I might ruffle a few feathers but I'm fair-minded and my actions are by the book. If somebody decides to try and punish me for taking my job seriously, then I must be doing something right."

"Absolutely."

Simon turned to walk down the stairs, but all this talk of going by the book had nudged Dani's memory.

"Oh wait up, Simon, I've been meaning to tell you that I tracked down the cop who called me at home—the one looking for a witness matching your description. I wanted to ask him why he hadn't filed an official request. Do you remember that I told you about him right after the shooting incident?"

He slowed on the stairs but didn't stop. "He was the cop from Nashville, right? Cory Nelson."

"Colin Nelson," she corrected. "From Memphis."

"Oh yeah, I remember now. What did you find out?"

"He's a legitimate detective all right. I found him in the police directory and gave him a call."

Simon now stopped and turned. "You spoke to him, huh?"

"I sure did, and you'll never guess what he told me."

"What?"

"He said that the witness he was trying to locate is now dead."

Simon swayed on the stair, which forced him to lean against the wall while he tried to steady his nerves.

"That's sad," he said. "Did the detective say how the guy died?"

"He was shot by the person he was meant to testify against," she said. "Detective Nelson made a mistake in thinking that the witness had relocated to Homer. Apparently, he'd never left Memphis and he was found dead just yesterday."

Simon scrambled for words that would make him appear calm and unflustered. Colin obviously couldn't make an official police request for information because the case involving the so-called witness didn't exist. When faced with

Dani's probing questions, he'd simply concocted a story to make the whole issue go away.

"What did I tell you?" he said, forcing a smile. "It's proof that we all have doppelgängers out there."

"I'm sorry if I seemed suspicious when I asked you about it," she said. "It's only because you matched the description down to the last detail."

"Like I already said, you don't have to apologize to me for asking questions."

She shuffled awkwardly as her gaze fell to her feet. "I kind of feel like I do owe you an apology," she said. "When I first met you, I wasn't sure if you were being entirely truthful with me. I didn't trust you and I was prickly."

"Do you trust me now?" he asked, not really wanting to know the answer. Whatever it was, it would cause him pain. He had neither earned nor warranted her trust, but he craved it so much.

"I think I *do* trust you," she said. "The way you've stepped up to help me out tells me a lot about the type of person you are. I'm glad you've moved into Homer because we need more people like you. You've got a good sense of community spirit. If you stick around, our little town will take hold of your heart and never let go."

Although he knew they were based on a lie, he allowed Dani's words to lift and inspire him. This was what he'd craved ever since beginning his custodial sentence—community, neighborliness, a town to call his own. When his cell door had clanged shut sixteen years ago, he had been surrounded by hostile forces, chanting his name, hammering on the bars with metal cups to let him know that cops were especially hated in prison ranks. It had taken him a good couple of years to convince the other inmates to accept him. He'd narrowly escaped being stabbed on a couple of occasions. It had been awful, but God's promise of grace had sustained him and allowed him to finally thrive in prison and even make friends. He felt the Lord's strength flowing into his veins when he was at his lowest ebb, encouraging him to endure the hardship and keep the faith.

"I hope I can prove that I'm worthy of the trust you've put in me, Dani," he said. "But whatever happens, I want you to know that I care about you."

She smiled. "I care about you too, Simon."

He continued his way downstairs, the weight of the world pressing hard on his shoulders. If his situation were different, the closeness that was growing between him and Dani would be a cause for joy. In reality though, he was a pretender with a secret so horrible that his life was destined to be lived alone. Who would want him in their community if his story ever came out?

Not the chief of police, that was for sure.

FIVE

Dani drove along the Sterling Highway, the only road that led in and out of Homer. It was mostly quiet at this time of year, except for the occasional moose or bear that wandered across the asphalt. The wide-open landscape was all she'd ever known, having been born and raised in Homer, like her mother and grandmother before her. The forests and mountains and sweet clapboard stores that lined The Spit filled her with pleasure. This was her home, her safe haven. Trey had tried to destroy it for her, but she had only come back stronger. She could see why Simon had taken such a shine to it.

She pondered on Simon Walker as she drove. No matter how hard she'd tried to be wary of him, he had proven himself to be reliable, considerate and good-hearted. Whenever she'd pressed Trey for details on his life before her, he'd insisted that his background was too dull and boring to discuss. Simon was different. Despite clearly wanting privacy, he had tried to reassure her of his integrity, giving her those small details about his life willingly. They weren't exactly ground-shaking facts, but for someone as closed off as Simon, it was a big deal.

"He's not like Trey," she said out loud, trying to convince herself. "He's a much better man than that."

She'd been certain that she wouldn't consider getting close to a man unless she knew every detail of his life, but she was breaking that rule little by little every day. Before she knew what she was doing, she was imagining Simon putting his arms around her waist and smiling down at her, creating those small dimples in his orange stubble and cute creases around his green eyes.

"Stop it, Dani," she admonished herself. "Just because he fixed your gutters doesn't mean you gotta drag him down the aisle."

She turned her truck onto The Homer Spit, the long stretch of land that jutted out into Kachemak Bay, where she liked to stroll on Saturdays, browsing the artisan stores that lined the popular shopping locale. The Spit was a tourist trap in the summer months, but even in winter it could be busy with locals. Not today though. Today was bitterly cold, with a mottled overhead sky and a thin mist hanging in the air. Technically, she wasn't meant to be back at work, having promised her doctor that she'd take the recommended two weeks of medical leave to recover from her brain injury. But after seven days, she was getting cabin fever, shut up in that house with nothing to look forward to except daily video calls from her mom and Mia. Simon also called her every day with some excuse about needing to know what thickness of loft insulation she'd like or if her window frames required repainting, but she guessed he just wanted to talk and check up on her.

Dani enjoyed his calls but she simply wasn't getting enough stimulation locked away in her home. She had an important investigation to continue and that's exactly why she was there at The Spit. She had plans to call on the Franklins at the fancy restaurant they'd recently opened—the one they splashed all over social media at every opportunity.

Pulling up outside The Kenai Cove, Dani immediately noticed a white moving van on the road with its doors open, the inside empty as if awaiting cargo. Two men were standing on the boardwalk outside the restaurant, both big and burly like nightclub bouncers. They were arguing with the restaurant owners—

Nick and Sonia Franklin—and Sonia's brother Kyle Mitchell.

"Hey," she said, exiting her truck and pulling on her beanie. "What's going on here?"

Kyle looked across at her and she saw his eyes narrow. "That's none of your business, Chief. We're attending to some personal matters here."

"When personal matters involve creating a disturbance in a public place, then it becomes a police matter too," she said. "I'll ask you for a second time—what's going on here?"

Kyle's face darkened and he opened his mouth to speak but his sister put a finger on his lips to silence him before walking toward Dani. Sonia looked terrible, with dark rings under her eyes and her mass of dark curls looking frizzy and unkempt beneath the scarf that she'd tied over her head. She'd also lost weight, which wasn't really surprising under the circumstances.

"We've got a cash flow issue at the restaurant," Sonia said, arms tightly crossed against her parka jacket. "These men have come to either collect what we owe or repossess some of our kitchen equipment. We're paying them the total due in cash, but they're adding a lot of fees on top, so we got into a disagreement."

Dani looked behind Sonia to where Nick

was counting out bills into the hand of one of the repo men. Kyle, meanwhile, still stared at Dani through narrowed eyes. A couple of years back, Kyle had been medically discharged from the army after suffering a head injury during a training exercise. He now took medication to control the seizures that he suffered as a result, and he'd sunk his military compensation payment into The Kenai Cove, partnering with Sonia and Nick in this new business venture.

"I hear you got hit in the head during a home invasion," Sonia said with surprising compassion. "Shouldn't you be taking some time off work?" She glanced over her shoulder. "Kyle was never the same after his head trauma. It's probably best to wait until the doctors give you the all clear."

"I'm fine. Totally recovered. I'm not here to talk about me, Sonia. I'm here to ask you some more questions about Jade, but it looks like you're in a tricky situation at the moment. What kind of financial difficulties are you having? Is it serious?"

"No, not at all. We're having a hard time because all our resources have gone into finding Jade." Her eyes suddenly became steely. "It doesn't help when you send Jordy over to our house with a warrant to search her room. Why can't you leave us alone, Dani? We've cooperated every step of the way, but you keep casting doubt on us and making us out to be liars."

Dani sighed. "I'm not trying to make you feel attacked, Sonia, but your cooperation has been sporadic and something doesn't feel quite right. In the last six weeks, you've been continuing your blogs and podcasts and social media marketing for the restaurant. It looks like all your efforts have gone into your business rather than finding Jade."

Sonia raised her voice. "How dare you! This restaurant is our only income. When we find Jade, she'll need a roof over her head and food on the table, so we have to keep going. What else can we do?"

Dani dropped her gaze to the ground, a little humbled by these words. In a flash, Kyle was by his sister's side. Meanwhile, the repo men returned to their van to shut up the doors, apparently satisfied with their payment.

"Is the chief upsetting you, sis?" Kyle asked, placing a protective arm around Sonia's shoulder. "You don't have to talk to her, you know. The reason we're in this mess with money is because of her." He jabbed a finger in Dani's face, directly in line with her nose. "Almost every cent we make is funding a private detective to find Jade. That's why we've got bailiffs knocking on the door. It's all your fault."

"That's not fair, Kyle," Dani said, gently pushing away the finger that was just an inch away. "I'm as determined to find Jade as you are, but I have to explore every single avenue, and I don't think that Sonia and Nick are being totally truthful with me."

Overhearing this comment, Nick shook his head and placed his hands on his hips. He was a large man with both a big appetite and big personality that made him popular with everyone—Dani included. Over the years, she had often stopped for coffee at the fast-food cabin he used to run on the highway before opening this more upscale restaurant. The friendship they'd developed had become strained since Jade's disappearance.

"Just what do you think we're keeping from you, Dani?" he called. "We told you everything you want to know."

"Yeah, but the details keep changing," she said. "At first you said that Jade took her cell phone to school but then you said she'd lost it the day before. You've also told us that in the days leading to her disappearance, you saw a prowler, a suspicious vehicle and some cigarette butts beneath her bedroom window. It feels like you're sending us on wild-goose chases to keep us from discovering the truth about what happened."

"The truth is that my little girl has been taken by a stranger," Nick yelled, throwing his hands in the air. "And she's out there somewhere while you're here, wasting time by harassing us."

Dani remained calm. "Why did you prevent us from searching her room without a warrant? What didn't you want us to find?"

Sonia pinched the bridge of her nose. "If we want to keep Jade's bedroom a private space for her, then that's our business. Getting a search warrant was mean and hurtful."

"I'm sorry you were hurt by it, but I'm the police chief and I have a job to do."

"And we also have a job to do," Sonia shot back. "I don't want you here at our restaurant, scaring away the customers. I'd like you to leave."

"There's a couple of things I need to ask first," Dani protested. "It won't take a moment."

"Get outta here!" Kyle yelled as he was joined by Nick. "We're done talking to you."

"No more questions," Nick shouted, pointing to the road. "Get back in your truck and go find my daughter."

Dani held up her hands in a gesture of appeasement to try to de-escalate the situation, but it was too late. The commotion had attracted the attention of other store owners, who spilled out onto the sidewalk to watch the drama. One of these owners, Adam Gleeson, came running from his trinket store, yanking on a jacket.

"Hey, hey!" he shouted. "Break it up." He pulled on Nick's shoulder. "Leave the chief alone, guys."

Sonia turned with her chin in the air and stalked into the restaurant.

"Let's go inside," she said, encouraging her family to follow. "Brawling on the street isn't a good look for a classy establishment like ours."

As Dani watched them disappear into their restaurant, she heaved a sigh and leaned heavily on the hood of her police truck. She'd totally messed up. Now, the Franklins would be even more uncooperative. Still, it was good to hear that Jordy had searched Jade's room. That might provide some clues. She should get to the station.

"Everything okay?" Adam asked, glancing between her and The Kenai Cove. "What was that all about?"

"I can't discuss the investigation with you, Adam. It's confidential."

"Sonia told me that you got a search warrant

and sent Jordy to ransack Jade's bedroom," he said. "Is that true?"

She stood upright. "The police don't ransack anything. We search methodically and carefully for clues to help us solve the crime."

By the look on Adam's face, he wasn't buying it.

"From what the Franklins say, you haven't been doing much of that," he said. "I've been defending you when they bad-mouth you, but it's starting to look like they've got a point. What are you doing here on The Spit when you should be out looking for Jade?"

Dani's reply was slow and deliberate. "I can't look for Jade until I know where she went."

Adam flared his nostrils. "Well, one thing's for sure, you ain't gonna find her here, are you?"

"You'd be surprised where missing kids turn up," she replied coolly. "Have you noticed anything unusual about Nick and Sonia's behavior lately? Have any strange vehicles or suspicious people visited their restaurant?"

"Are you accusing them of having something to do with their daughter's abduction?" he asked incredulously. "Because that's what it sounds like."

"I'm not accusing anybody of anything. I'm trying to establish the facts."

"The Franklins are distraught," Adam said, sounding indignant. "Haven't they been through enough without you making it worse? You've always been well-liked in this town, Chief, but plenty of people aren't happy with the way you're handling this investigation."

"I didn't join the police force to win any popularity contests," she said, getting into her truck and slamming the door.

Switching on the engine, she turned the truck around and headed for the station, while the store owners on The Spit silently faded into the sea mist in her rearview mirror.

Simon cupped his hands around his eyes and placed his forehead against the cold window, peering into Dani's living room and discovering no one was there. As usual, her rocking chair was neatly aligned with the television, a colorful crocheted blanket folded over the armrest. He guessed that, along with the house, she had inherited her grandmother's furniture. The velour couches, dark wood dresser and china figurines weren't something he'd expect a woman in her midthirties to choose for her home. Perhaps this house had given her an opportunity to get rid of the belongings she'd once shared with her husband and fully erase the legacy of her disastrous marriage. He knew how painful it was to be surrounded by memories of a life that was long gone. It was why he abandoned literally everything in Memphis and left with just the clothes on his back. A fresh start sure wasn't for the fainthearted, but sometimes it was necessary.

He skirted around the house and knocked on the back door, only to receive no answer. It was clear that Dani had gone out, despite still being on medical leave. He wasn't so worried about her physical health as her safety. Since the latest attack on her, Simon had thought about her well-being constantly. It was why he'd been phoning every day, under the guise of helping with house maintenance. Except today she hadn't picked up.

Since he'd learned the name of the man who was likely behind the attacks on her, he'd done a little online research. Based on what he'd found out, Freddy Lomax wasn't exactly a criminal genius. While out on bail awaiting his trial fifteen years ago, Lomax had photographed himself outside the gutted Anchorage warehouse, laughing and pointing at the destruction, before uploading the images to his social media account. Yes, he was apparently *that* stupid. The calculated actions of Dani's attacker didn't seem to align with Lomax's low intellect.

Simon returned to his truck, where Lola waited patiently on the front seat, her breath steaming up the passenger window. Maybe he should take a quick drive to the police station to see if Dani was there. He was finding it difficult to stay away from her, but the last thing he wanted was to make her feel stifled, especially since she was the chief of police and he was just a handyman neighbor.

Turning the key in the ignition, he decided to go to the hardware store in town and place an order for the insulation that Dani's loft space required. He didn't mind paying for it and giving her the option of reimbursing him in installments. He knew she would never allow him to fully fund her home improvements, but the expense might prove too much to manage in one go, and he'd recently received a large payment for three matching cabinets he'd built for a client. If he happened to drive by the police station while he made his way to the hardware store, he could check the parking lot for her truck. There was no harm in that, right? He wouldn't be crowding her and it would put his mind at rest to know she was safe with her colleagues.

The drive into town was, as always, a joy, even in this gray, misty weather. The snow that fell in Homer over the winter months made it an ideal location for skiers, snowboarders and skaters. Simon loved the outdoor lifestyle that the area promoted and he'd started fishing on the quieter shores of the bay, catching the most amazing halibut he'd ever eaten. He also liked to hike in the Kenai Mountains, taking Lola for company and sometimes camping out overnight in his small tent. It hadn't taken long for him to decide that Homer was where he belonged, and he wanted desperately to be able to stay and keep it as his long-term home.

Remaining in the area depended on keeping a low profile. Driving into Homer made him realize just how difficult a task this might prove. He'd already made many acquaintances in this town, and several people waved at him from the sidewalk. He couldn't call them friends, not yet, but his reputation for crafting unique and stylish pieces of furniture had brought him to the attention of residents. He had made plenty of baby cribs, coffee tables, bookcases and even a bow and arrow set as a special gift for a local archer. He had learned the trade while in prison, reveling in the pleasure it brought him to create something with his own two hands. His shop instructor had noticed his talent for carpentry early on, and had requested extra time and resources from the prison warden in order to teach him more complex skills. By the time of his release, Simon was an expert in the craft, having had fifteen long years to master the techniques. That invaluable experience now allowed him to earn a living without having to apply for a regular job, where he might be required to disclose his conviction. Working alone was his preference these days.

Slowing to a crawl as he approached the police station, Simon scanned the parking lot for Dani's truck. It wasn't there, but Jordy was standing by the door of the building, a small crowd of people gathered around him. The officer appeared to be trying to placate the group, using body language that Simon recognized as a de-escalating technique: head up, shoulders back, hands by his side. Something was wrong here. He pulled into a spot, exited the vehicle and went to join the throng.

"She's bad for business," a woman was saying. "We don't want her on The Spit causing trouble anymore."

"It looks like she doesn't have control of the investigation," a bearded man said. "She pretty much told me to my face that she thinks Nick and Sonia are guilty of something."

"Let's all take a minute to calm down," Jordy said. "I'm sure that the chief will be happy to address your concerns as soon as she gets back."

"Hey, y'all," Simon shouted above the chatter. "Does anybody know where Dani is right now?"

"She left The Spit a half hour ago," the man next to him said, the only person to reply. "Some of us store owners decided to come here and have a discussion with her about the way she's harassing Nick and Sonia. We're like a family on The Spit and we stick up for each other."

"She owes the Franklins an apology," someone else shouted. "We know she's hiding from us in there. That's why you won't let us inside."

"The chief isn't supposed to be working today," Jordy called out. "She's meant to be resting after an injury so let's cut her some slack. I promise you that she's not here, but I'll ask her to look into your concerns when she checks in to the station."

Voices of dissent grew louder, the townsfolk apparently dissatisfied with this response.

"Listen, everybody." Jordy now raised his hands to try to quieten everyone. "Chief Pearce has been placed on medical leave, so she might not be acting like her usual self. If she's upset any of you, I'm sure she'll want to smooth things over as soon as possible."

"You're just as bad as she is, Jordy," a woman called. "You're doing her dirty work by trawling through Jade's room and invading that poor family's privacy. It's obscene."

"That search was necessary in order to thoroughly investigate Jade's disappearance," Jordy said. "I haven't yet had the opportunity to share my findings with Chief Pearce, so please don't talk about this matter with her until she's been officially cleared to return to work."

"Too late," a man shouted. "I already told her that you'd ransacked the room."

Jordy ran a hand down his face. "That's the wrong choice of words, Adam. We're on your side here. Please try to remember that."

Simon had heard enough. He turned and ran back to his truck before starting it up and immediately heading out onto the road leading to The Spit. He knew that Dani was desperate to hear any details relating to the search of Jade's bedroom. In their phone conversations, she'd let slip a couple of times that she was hoping a new lead might be generated by examining the room. If she'd learned that Jordy had completed the search, she would have headed straight for the station. And if these store owners had arrived before she did, that could only mean one thing: she'd been prevented from getting there.

Lola seemed to sense the anxiety he exuded and whined a little as he drove. She put her paws up on the dash to follow the road ahead. It was eventually her bark that alerted him to something that he would otherwise have missed. The road to The Spit was narrow, protruding out into the bay with the lapping ocean on either side. The banks leading to the water's edge were only a few feet in length but steep enough to overturn a vehicle that lost control. And that's exactly what seemed to have happened to Dani. There, sunk into the water, was her truck, lying on its roof with all four tires breaking the surface like periscopes.

"No, no, no," he said, slamming on his brakes to come to a sudden stop on the asphalt.

He jumped from the truck and scrambled down the rocky bank, with Lola at his side. He then plunged into the icy water, the temperature momentarily taking his breath away. A persistent wind whipped across the sea with the force of thousands of needles, stinging his cheeks, but he forced his face below the surface using the side-view mirror as leverage to hold himself under. Lola yelped and barked on the shoreline, her cries muffled beneath the surface as he fumbled in the murkiness, feeling his way around. The driver's window was fully down, allowing him to swim inside and ensure that the interior was empty. Dani wasn't there.

When he broke through the shallow water and took a huge lungful of air, Lola began to pace back and forth on the stones, a behavior she only displayed when she wanted to follow a trail. She'd detected a scent. He pulled out his cell phone from his jacket pocket to call the police. The screen flickered and flashed and refused to cooperate when he attempted to unlock it. The internal electronics must have been damaged by the salt water. In his haste to save Dani, he'd failed to call for help before plunging into the ocean. That was a rookie error that proved how much he'd forgotten of his training over the last fifteen years.

He began to shiver, following Lola along the waterline. He was sopping wet, being buffeted by the surging winds sweeping across the bay, and he made efforts to slow his rapid breathing. That would allow him more control over his trembling. But he would still need to warm up his body soon to prevent hypothermia setting in. Lola ran on ahead, her paws hopping across the large stones that lined the shore, leaving wet prints behind as she strayed into shallow water. Something had clearly piqued her interest and she sniffed her way forward, occasionally looking back to check that her master was following.

"What is it, girl?" he encouraged when she stopped and began to bark. "What did you find?"

The dog nuzzled her face between two large rocks and grasped something in her jaws, yanking it out with a powerful tug. He ran to her and took the item from her mouth. It was a black shoe, size five, standard-issue police footwear. It had to be Dani's. Perhaps she'd gotten it caught as she'd scaled the bank, trying to reach the road. Had someone been pursuing her, perhaps?

"Go on, Lola." Simon made a motion for her to continue on the trail. "Lead the way."

She responded instantly, scrambling up the steep bank and reaching the road in just a few seconds. By now, Simon was struggling to maintain his usual levels of strength and his limbs were numb and unresponsive as he hauled himself up the stones. He'd only been in the water for a minute or two but he needed to return to his car and warm up within a half hour. The highway above was quiet and he guessed that many of the store owners were still at the police station. He needed to assess how far he could realistically follow Lola on the trail before turning back to his vehicle and its warming vents.

Mustering his strength to heave himself onto the road, he stood and breathed hard while he doubled over with his hands on his knees. In one direction was his truck and in the other, the lights of The Spit were faintly visible in the fog. Between those two points was nothing but the whistling wind and a straight, empty road.

"Find her," he said to his hound as she sniffed the road and located a scent that led to The Spit. "I'm right behind you."

Gritting his teeth to prevent them from chattering, he started to jog, praying that Lola was following a trail created by the running of Dani's steps and not by the dragging of her body.

SIX

Dani tore open one of the cardboard boxes in the small storage shed that belonged to a surfwear clothing store. Yanking out a bright yellow sweatshirt, she pulled it over her head as best she could with violently shaking hands. Her body was so cold that pain tore through her limbs and the skin on her shoeless foot was burning as if scalded. She took out another sweatshirt, wrapped it around her foot and tried to wiggle her toes beneath the thick cotton but they were uncooperative, unable to feel a thing through the numbness. Hearing a noise somewhere outside, she sank to the floor and wedged herself between two stacks of boxes before hugging her knees and rocking slightly. Without knowing who had run her off the road, she was wary of asking for help from someone unknown, and nearly all of the stores now seemed to be closed.

She was without her gun, radio and cell

phone—all of which she stored safely in her glove box while driving. When her truck had flipped into the water, the force of the impact had popped open the glove box and allowed everything to fall beneath the surface. She had spent at least ten minutes searching for the items to no avail. Meanwhile a long line of vehicles had rumbled on the road overhead. She was pretty certain that this sudden rush of traffic from The Spit had saved her life. Her attacker obviously couldn't finish the job while people were around, and she'd tried to take her chance to flag down one of the cars. But scaling that steep bank had proved a lot harder than it looked, and she'd gotten her foot caught, eventually being forced to leave her shoe between two rocks. By the time she reached the road, it was deserted. Not even the white van that had forced her off the road was in sight. And The Spit was her only hope of calling for help.

But when she'd reached the nearest store, the closed sign was visible through the glass on the door—and before she could move on, she'd realized she was being tracked. Someone was weaving between the wooden clapboard buildings, a shadowy figure in the mist, flitting in and out of her vision in a way that made her question whether she could trust her own eyesight. The surf store's outbuilding was her best chance of staying out of view and she had never been more thankful to find that the owner hadn't changed his padlock code since an attempted break-in the previous year. She couldn't even be angry with him for the lax security.

Now inside the small storage unit, Dani felt anything but safe. Shivering wildly and sensing the early stages of hypothermia setting in, she pressed her forehead to her knees and mentally replayed the crash: a white van, no time to react, a clip to her bumper, the sudden and terrifying impact of the water, the windshield cracking like a thunderbolt.

She lifted her head, holding her breath. There were footsteps very close by, slowly shuffling on the boardwalk as if in no particular hurry. Straining to hear, she wondered whether it could be Paul, the surf store owner, who always wore sandals that dragged across the ground as he walked. Or was it her attacker, casually searching the area without a care in the world? She hated this feeling of not knowing whom to trust, of being totally reliant on someone to come save her. She hadn't experienced this degree of helplessness since that first night after Trey's arrest, when she'd sat and cradled her swollen belly, praying to

God that the not-yet-born baby girl wouldn't suffer because of her father's wrongdoing.

It was thoughts of Trey that galvanized her and forced her to get up. She would not be a victim again. She was a fighter, and she would protect herself as best she could. Ripping open more boxes, she searched for something she could use as a weapon. Casting aside piles of clothing, wetsuits and snorkels, her eye was drawn to a glint on the floor as she moved a box. A box cutter had been left behind and she quickly grabbed it and struggled to slide the blade out of the top with her numb, trembling fingers. Her fine motor movement was in terrible shape, and the urgency to find warmth was becoming critical. Inching to the door while dragging her sweatshirt-covered foot behind her, she listened for sounds of the person outside.

Nothing.

Lifting the latch as quietly as possible, she cracked open the door just a couple of inches. When the wind gusted through the gap, she gasped, realizing that further exposure to the elements would give her only minutes to find warm shelter before there would be serious consequences. The Kenai Cove advertised their cozy interior and open fire on their signage outside, and it was only a few doors away.

Would the Franklins take pity on her and allow access to their restaurant? Or would they abandon her to her fate in light of their earlier argument? She would have to take the risk.

Clutching the handle of her box cutter, she took a step onto the wooden planks and tried to force her body to stop shivering. The mist descending on The Spit had grown thicker, swirling almost like smoke around the boardwalk that extended into the sea on long, thin stilts. The harbor on the opposite side of the road was full of docked boats but quiet, the only sounds coming from the cawing gulls and wind chimes. But someone else was there with her. She sensed him before she saw him—a menacing presence just waiting for her to reveal herself.

A figure appeared through the mist, dark like a shadow but perfectly solid when its hands curled themselves around her throat from the side. Instinctively, she swung her arms, waving the box cutter through the air, trying to make contact with any part of his body. Her body was weak, all her strength having been sapped by the hypothermic state that was settling into her muscles. She was in no condition to defend herself and knew it.

So did he.

"Please, stop," she said, as the hands moved from her throat to around her waist and picked her up effortlessly before throwing her against the side of the storage unit where she crumpled to the ground. "This won't help you, Freddy. Think of your future."

Sliding to the floor, Dani thought she saw him pause for a moment to listen. Had she correctly identified this man as Freddy Lomax? And was he responding to her attempts to engage with him on a personal level? Hoping that was the case, she persevered with the dialogue.

"You served your time, Freddy," she said, pushing herself onto all fours, her arms trembling with the effort. "Don't do anything stupid and end up back in prison. If you leave now and never come back, you'll be safe. I can't positively ID you yet, so we can still pretend this never happened."

It was certainly true that she couldn't identify him, given his attire. Dressed in black cargo pants, an oversize military-style jacket, ski mask and trapper hat, he was more like a yeti than a person. And in his right hand, she now saw a knife—small-handled and short-bladed like a dagger.

"Stop," she yelled, seeing him loom over her, the blade striking toward her arm. "I'll defend myself."

Swinging her box cutter with abandon, she managed to repel his attack, summoning all the reserves of energy in her body. She imagined Mia playing with her trucks or dolls right at that moment, and the images gave her strength. Her daughter needed her to survive. She would not go down without a fight.

A bark took them both by surprise, causing her attacker to jump backward and freeze. Seemingly emerging from out of nowhere, Simon's dog, Lola, launched herself across the boardwalk, taking flight and landing right in front of Dani before barking furiously. The dog's bark was deep and loud and howling, creating the most intimidating sound that Dani had ever heard. It was enough to send her attacker turning and running at top speed, obviously deciding that he'd met his match in Lola.

Dani rested her hand on Lola's back, using the dog's sturdy weight as a leaning post to help her stand.

"Where's your master?" she said, her breath rasping in short, sharp puffs. "He's gotta be close."

Sure enough, Simon appeared within seconds, guided by Lola's deep howls. When he saw Dani, he rushed to her and took her face in his hands to check her over for injuries, just like she might do with Mia. He was wet and shaking too, his skin as ashen as hers felt.

Quieting the dog with a head pat and a word

of praise, he said to Dani, "Let's get you some-place warm. Hold on to my arm and don't let go."

She grabbed hold of him and leaned heavily. She'd never been so glad to see anybody in her life, and she tried to speak but no words would come. Instead her teeth began to chatter uncontrollably as the adrenaline faded along with her strength. She figured that her muteness was a good thing anyway because if she could have spoken, she would've told him that she loved him, whether it was true or not.

Simon and Dani sat by the hearth in the lounge at The Kenai Cove, holding their palms to the glow of the flames with splayed fingers. Lola was curled on the rug by their feet, snoring peacefully while sleeping off the day's dramatic events, oblivious to the fact she was a lifesaving hero. Simon reached down and scratched her belly for the umpteenth time, giving her all the attention she deserved. She stretched out her paws, yawned and blinked her eyes open sleepily. He was sure he saw her lips turn up in a little smile.

The Franklins had been shocked to see Simon and Dani burst through the door two hours ago, soaked to the bone and shivering wildly, but they had immediately been hospitable, providing hot, sweet coffee and calling the police station to request help. Sonia Franklin had even allowed Lola inside too, but had insisted all three of them remain in the lounge and well away from the restaurant. Simon didn't mind being relegated to the lounge. It was tastefully furnished and comfortable, with plush velvet sofas and ornate rugs, lit from above by huge glass chandeliers. The soft jazz that played in the background added to the ambience, but the place was almost empty, with just one family eating in the restaurant. He wondered whether lunchtimes were usually this quiet or if the business was struggling.

"I look like a blancmange," Dani said, pulling at the fluffy pink sweater she wore over lilac sweatpants. "I don't want to sound ungrateful, but I'm sure that Sonia gave me the ugliest clothes she could find."

"If you don't want to sound ungrateful then I'd suggest smiling and saying thank you. The Franklins could've turned us away. And if they had, I don't know where we could have gone when everyplace else was closed. We're alive thanks to them."

"Yeah." Dani nodded sheepishly. "You're right. A bright pink sweater is much better than my cold, wet uniform." She turned her body toward his on the sofa. "You never got a change of clothes though. Are you sure you're okay?"

"I'm fine."

On their arrival, Sonia had found some old clothes for Dani and allowed her to use the staff shower to warm up. But Simon couldn't leave Lola alone in the lounge so he had stood in front of the fire for an hour, turning himself like a chicken on a spit as the steam rose from the fabric of his jeans and T-shirt. He had now dried to a stiff crisp, like laundry in hot sun. His clothes gave off a briny smell, salty and earthy like the shells he used to collect on his childhood vacations in Florida. He remembered running barefoot on the sand, seeking his favorite type of shell—the kind which allowed you to hear the ocean waves crashing in the hollow.

"You smell like the beach," Dani said, nudging him with her elbow.

"Seaweed or ice cream?" he joked.

"Seaweed."

He laughed. "I need to go home and take a hot shower," he said. "Do you know how much longer Jordy and Vernon will be?"

"Let's give them another twenty minutes. They asked us to stay until they've made their inquiries so we should give them a little more time."

Vernon and Jordy had responded instantly to the call for help and had set about phoning as many of The Spit's store owners as they could, trying to get a lead on the white van that had run Dani off the road. The problem was that it was a standard cargo van—the same kind that plenty of small-business owners used in Homer. The local rentals firm had a fleet of them too. Due to the suddenness of the incident and the speed at which the vehicle loomed, Dani had been unable to get a read on the plate or notice any identifying features.

"I definitely won't be leaving you here alone anyway," Simon said. "Somebody is really determined to hurt you."

Her face turned downcast. "It's hard to imagine what makes a person act with such hatred."

"If your testimony put this guy in jail for fourteen years then I guess he used all that time to grow bitter about it. Prison either makes or breaks a man. Or so I've heard."

"Yeah, well, if that's true then it definitely broke Freddy Lomax because he's unhinged." She shook her head. "I just wish I'd gotten a look at his face today. I really need to know for sure who I'm dealing with. I hate this feeling of being hunted. I just..." She shook her head. "I don't really have the words, actually.

It's hard to explain to someone who's never been through it."

"I think I've got a good idea how it feels," he said. "I'm sorry this is happening to you."

He stared at the floor, thinking about the similarities to his own situation. He and Dani were more alike than she realized: both stalked by men with a grudge and forced to take desperate actions to defend themselves. Except plenty of people would support the Peterson brothers in taking him down, whereas Dani was an innocent victim of a violent criminal. He could never hope to be considered innocent and was definitely not a victim in most people's opinion.

"I'm not actually meant to be back at work yet," she said after a long silence. "Vernon devised a whole schedule for me to be constantly partnered with a colleague once I was back on duty in order to keep me safe." She rolled her eyes. "And he's pretty sore that I went out on a lone patrol and put myself in danger."

"He's got a point, Dani," Simon said. "What was so important that you had to come down to The Spit on your own anyway?"

She glanced across to the restaurant where Sonia was wiping a cloth across a table. Dani and Sonia were clearly not comfortable with each other and despite the Franklins initial hospitality, he'd gotten the feeling that they were pretty eager for their unexpected guests to leave.

"I wanted to ask Sonia and Nick some questions about Jade," she said quietly, her hand placed across her mouth, presumably to avoid being lip-read by an eagle-eyed Sonia. "But it didn't go too well and we ended up having an argument on the street."

"Yeah, I heard about it at the police station. Arguing isn't going to help matters, is it?"

"Tell me about it. Sometimes I think I should've been a lawyer instead of a cop. I'm always arguing my case."

"And that's what I love about you." He stopped abruptly and reddened, covering his embarrassment with a cough. "I mean that's what I admire about you. You don't suffer fools."

She threw back her head and laughed, long and hard, almost bitterly.

"I suffered the biggest fool in the world," she said finally. "That's probably why I'm so determined not to do it again. Fool me once, shame on you. Fool me twice and I'll hunt you down with a baseball bat until the end of time."

They both laughed in sync, natural and easy, as though they'd known each other for years. Simon was enjoying this time with Dani way too much, despite knowing that their closeness was all based on lies.

"You're a good guy, Simon," she said, her clear blue eyes locking onto his. "What my dad would call the salt of the earth."

He looked down at his ocean-stiffened clothes. "Literally, I think."

"Can I be serious for a second?" she said, taking his hand. "You've been there for me plenty of times lately and I want to say thank you. We make a pretty good team, don't you think?"

The warmth of her hand on his was exquisite, but he withdrew it, a sudden wave of guilt and nausea washing over him. The lies he'd endlessly told coursed through his veins, poisoning his blood, making his words stick in his throat. He longed to be free of the deceit.

"What's up?" she asked. "Did I say something wrong?"

"No." He laced his fingers together and leaned forward on his knees, staring into the flames. "I'm not the man you think I am, Dani, and I'll only end up disappointing you if we get any closer."

She searched his face. "What do you mean? If you're not the man I think you are, then who are you?"

"I'm... I'm..."

Could he really do this? Taking a deep breath, he prepared himself, only to be interrupted by

Kyle Mitchell, wearing chef's pants and a tunic, carrying a steaming bowl of French fries.

"I thought you guys might be hungry," he said, placing the bowl on the side table. "These are on the house." He nodded at Dani. "You okay, Chief Pearce? My sister told me what happened. I hope they find the guy responsible. I know we don't always see eye to eye, but you should be able to do your job without being attacked."

Dani looked up at Kyle, clearly surprised. "Thanks. I appreciate the support. And the fries."

"Sure thing. You got any leads on the suspect? You want some help with the investigation?"

"Thanks for the offer, Kyle, but my officers have got it covered."

"Right. Of course."

He turned and headed back to the kitchen, leaving behind an aroma of hot potatoes, salt and vinegar. Simon's mouth watered and he realized how famished he was. It was the hunger that brought him back to his senses, and it reminded him of all that he had to lose in Homer if he revealed too much.

"What were you about to say?" Dani asked as he reached for the bowl to place it on the couch between them. "It sounded important."

"I was about to say that I'm not the solid, sensible man you think I am," he said, making a swirling motion with his index finger at his temple. "I'm a little screwed up in the head after my divorce. I don't want you to think that I'm somebody special, when I'm really an emotional wreck."

He saw her features slide into a downcast expression, his words having successfully repelled any further probing. Yet he could see that his words had also hurt her, likely because he had rejected her at the very moment that she was beginning to open up.

"You don't have to worry about letting me down gently," she said, defensiveness creeping into her voice. "When I said we make a good team, I didn't mean as husband and wife. I think you misread where I was coming from."

"Of course I did," he said with a smile, hopelessly trying to lighten the mood. "That's because I'm an emotional wreck, remember?"

She did not return his smile, but picked up a fry, broke it in half and angled her body away from his while she blew angrily on the rising steam.

Dani stood with Vernon in the foyer of The Kenai Cove, focusing on her surroundings so she wouldn't have to think about all the other problems piling onto her shoulders. The space itself was nice enough, though rather too ornate for her tastes. The Franklins had installed a marble fountain, a feature that Dani thought might be more at home in a Las Vegas casino than a Homer eatery. The Spit was known for its rustic nature and good home cooking, and she wondered whether Sonia and Nick had misjudged their plan to open a fancy restaurant.

"Listen, Chief," Vernon said. "We've got no leads on the van, I'm afraid. There are just too many of them in the town and tracking each one is impossible. There are no security cameras overlooking the area where the collision took place, and I figure that whoever was driving the vehicle will have taken it well away from here for repair. Even so, I've put out an alert to all repair shops to be on the lookout for this type of van with hood damage. We got a tow truck dragging your cruiser from the bay right now."

"Any leads on the whereabouts of Freddy Lomax?" she asked. "He's gotta be our guy. The way he tried to stab me in the arm tells me that he wants me to suffer. I was unarmed and totally exposed out there. He could've pushed the blade into my neck and walked away, but he chose to hurt me slowly. That's exactly what I'd expect from him."

"The last confirmed sighting of Lomax was in Anchorage two weeks ago," Vernon said. "Then he just dropped off the radar. I'm sorry, Chief, but he's like a shadow in the night. We've got nothing to work with."

Dani was disappointed. "Looks like we'll have to do some good old-fashioned detective work, huh, Sergeant? He can't hide forever. Did you come across anything else that might be useful?"

"Nothing related to your case," he said, glancing to the lounge, where Simon sat with Lola. "But I definitely turned up information that could be considered interesting."

The way he said this sentence put her on edge. "What are you talking about?"

"Somebody was walking up and down The Spit this morning, looking for a man who matches Simon's description. Several of the store owners were approached by the same guy, asking if they know of anybody who was six feet four with red hair and green eyes."

She instantly thought of Detective Colin Nelson and his search for a witness from Memphis. But that witness was now dead, so why was somebody still searching for him?

"Did the man have a photograph or a name?" she asked. "Did he say why he wanted to track this person down?"

"He claimed to be an old military friend from way back who'd lost touch after they served together. Apparently, his friend changed his name and moved to Homer to start a new life."

Dani sighed. This cover story didn't sound convincing. And if she wasn't buying it, she guessed that The Spit store owners hadn't either.

"Did anyone point him toward Simon?" she asked.

"Of course not," Vernon replied. "You know what folks are like around here. They don't rat on their own, and even though Simon is a newbie, he's well-liked. They closed ranks around him."

Dani nodded in appreciation, expecting nothing else from the residents of Homer. They'd closed ranks around her too after Trey had been imprisoned, blocking news trucks and reporters from gaining access to the lane leading to her home, refusing to answer any questions and shielding her on the street if she was approached. They had protected her just like they were now protecting Simon.

"A little while ago, there was a police detective from Memphis looking for a witness to a crime who happened to match Simon's description," she said. "That case has now stalled because the witness was murdered, but this matter has got to be related, right? Maybe the guy who was here today is a private detective who's investigating the case on behalf of an interested party."

"Why would a private detective go looking for a dead man?" Vernon asked skeptically. "It's a wild-goose chase."

She shrugged. "Could be that he hasn't heard that the witness has been murdered."

"Maybe," he said. "Or maybe there's another explanation."

She folded her arms as if readying herself for a blow. "Like what?"

"Like Simon Walker is a wanted criminal. I think our mystery man asking questions on The Spit today might be a bail bondsman or a bounty hunter, and he's using a cover story to not spook anybody."

Dani felt her heart sink, a cold slithering sensation that started in her chest and ended up in her belly. Simon had been her rock lately, always turning up when she needed him, providing support and practical assistance, making her feel cherished in so many ways. She didn't want to be wrong about him, but Vernon was forcing her to face the possibility that she was being fooled all over again.

"Simon isn't like Trey," she said, trying to

convince herself rather than Vernon. "He's different."

"I know that you and Simon have gotten close," Vernon said, showing surprising sensitivity by softening his tone. "He's charming and nice and lavishing all this positive attention on you."

"He's not lavishing anything on me, Vernon." She was defensive. "He's been helping me with my house maintenance, and he's come to my aid on more than one occasion. He's just being a good citizen."

Vernon raised one eyebrow. "Is he being a good citizen or a good con man?"

She felt the breath being knocked right out of her lungs. "You think he's a con man?" She paused. "Really?"

"I think it's an idea that you've been avoiding because you want Simon to be a good guy. You gotta think like a cop. Distance yourself from the situation and let the facts speak for themselves. What do you know about this man? I mean what do you *really* know?"

She opened her mouth to reply, but closed it again when she realized how little she had to offer in response.

"Nothing of substance," she said forlornly.

"Exactly."

Dani let her shoulders sag, accepting that

she had seen in Simon the man she wanted to see. Maybe he was someone else entirely.

"Do you really think he's got something to hide, Sergeant?" she asked, taking Vernon's advice and reverting to being a cop again. "If so, what do think it might be?"

"He's definitely hiding something," Vernon replied. "I just hope he didn't commit a serious crime. The piece with the policeman in Memphis doesn't make sense though. If he was looking for a fugitive, why wouldn't he tell you that? Why make up a story about a missing witness? Wouldn't he want our help to apprehend the suspect?" Vernon shook his head. "We don't have all the pieces yet. But sure as I'm standing here, there's *something* serious going on. And we need to figure out what it is, before someone gets hurt."

Dani swallowed away a powerful sense of foreboding. She was afraid of what she might uncover but even more afraid of being kept in the dark. She stole a glance at the man she'd come to think of as an ally and a friend.

"If Simon Walker is keeping secrets, I'll lay them wide open. I can promise you that."

SEVEN

Simon stood in front of his bathroom mirror, rolling his neck in circles and massaging the tender spots at his nape, where tension had built up and created knots. His anxiety level was through the roof.

He was in trouble.

While watching Dani and Vernon talk in the foyer of The Kenai Cove earlier that evening, Simon had been acutely aware of the way they'd looked at him. He saw confusion, suspicion and betrayal on Dani's face, and he'd become certain they were talking about him—that something had happened to cast doubt upon his cover story. He had tried to lip-read Vernon's words, but the sergeant was wise to him, covering his mouth frequently while he spoke or angling his head away. They went to great lengths to ensure that Simon would not overhear and this could only mean one thing—danger.

He turned off the faucet and splashed his face with the cool water that had filled the sink. While patting his skin dry, he studied his reflection. In that moment, he felt every single one of his forty-five years. They were etched into the lines on his forehead and around his mouth, peppered into his slightly graying hair, embedded into the shoulder twinge he felt whenever he raised his arm too quickly. That particular injury resulted from breaking up a nasty fight between two inmates, causing his shoulder to dislocate. He had never fully recovered.

Not from that—or from the rest of it.

He was a product of his past and would never escape it. His life story was knitted into his flesh and bones, starting with the silvery scar on his knee from falling from a tricycle as a child and ending with the purple bruise on his thigh, created when he was frantically searching in the submerged patrol truck for Dani. Every cell in his body told him who he was: Officer Gabriel Smith, SWAT Commander, weapons expert, undercover operative, convicted cop killer.

A knock at the front door caused him to groan in dismay. There was only one person who'd come to his home at this time of night: Dani. The way he'd left The Kenai Cove so abruptly had denied her the opportunity to question him, and she obviously wasn't going to let their unfinished business rest. He walked from the bathroom to the hallway in his old gray sweats and well-worn socks. If he'd known he'd be receiving visitors he would've made more of an effort with his clothes, but Dani would have to take him as she found him. He quickly practiced painting on a welcoming smile in front of the hallway mirror. If he could keep the conversation light, he had more chance of fending off her inquiries, whatever they might be.

He padded on the polished wooden floor, through to his open-plan living room with its secondhand couches, rugs and lamps. He adored each piece of furniture, knowing that it was his and his alone. After living in a tiny cell for fifteen years, his simple home felt like paradise, and he really didn't want to open the door to any negativity. But Dani was there, at the front door, peering through the frosted glass panel. She appeared to be wearing her police uniform instead of Sonia's bright pink sweater.

"Hi there," he said, swinging open the door to see both Dani and Vernon standing on his porch with the snowy vista behind them. "This is a surprise. You should've told me you were coming and I'd have rustled up a meal."

"This isn't a social call, Simon." Dani was unsmiling, as was Vernon. "I'm here on police business. Do you think you could accompany us to the station for an interview? We have some questions we'd like to ask."

His guard came up like a drawbridge. "It's kind of late, don't you think? Can't we talk here?"

"It's only eight thirty." She was emotionless. "I'd rather talk at the station where it can be recorded. We can drive you there and back."

He had no intention of going to a police station, not even if his life depended on it.

"What's this about, Dani?"

"A man is looking for you," she said flatly. "I don't know what's going on or whether Colin Nelson is telling me the truth about his witness in Memphis, but somebody is going to an awful lot of effort to track you down." She leaned in through the door. "And I want to know why." She pointed to the police truck parked in front of his cabin. "So let's go, buster."

"It's dark and cold and I'm not going anywhere." He knew that he was coming off as difficult, but self-preservation had kicked in. "I'm not under arrest, am I?"

"Not yet."

He moistened his lips, letting the weight

of those two words sink in. Dani was playing hardball here, imagining all kinds of bad things about him no doubt. The man searching for him in Homer was most likely a private detective hired by the Petersons—or maybe one of the Petersons themselves—and Simon could only hope that the residents had refused to cooperate. From what he'd learned about Homer, it was a close-knit town.

He held open the door. "You wanna come in? I'll talk here, and that's my final offer."

Dani stepped onto the mat and turned to her sergeant. "I think it's best if I conduct this interview by myself, Vernon. Could you wait in the car? Keep the engine running and turn on the heat."

Vernon eyed Simon warily. "Sure thing, Chief. Holler if you need me and I'll come running."

Simon tried not to allow this comment to sting, but it was impossible. Just what did Vernon think he was capable of? He would never hurt anybody, least of all Dani. He cared about her way more than the sergeant could imagine. He shut the door and gestured to the couch, close to where a fire was roaring in the hearth. Lola was there, stretched out on the rug.

"Would you like a coffee?" he asked. "Or some juice?"

"No, thank you." She held up a phone in her hand. "Do you mind if I record our discussion?"

He settled himself in the chair opposite. "Okay by me, but this feels kinda hostile. I thought we were friends."

"Yeah, I thought so too, but that was before I started to suspect that you were lying to me." She took a jerky inhalation of breath. "I was just starting to care about you. I thought I could trust you. After everything I went through with Trey, I can't believe I allowed myself to be fooled by a man again."

In all of these words, one sentence resonated. "Did you say you were just starting to care about me?"

She placed two fingertips on her forehead and closed her eyes, as if disappointed in herself for revealing too much.

"This isn't easy for me," she said finally. "I've allowed my feelings for you to become complicated and I'm putting a stop to it right now. I suspect that you haven't been truthful with me and I'd like some honest answers about the man walking The Spit today, looking for somebody matching your description." She held up a preemptive hand. "And don't try and sidetrack me with the story about everybody having doppelgängers out there. There's only one redheaded man of six feet four living in Homer, and that's you."

This would seem like an ideal time to come clean, telling Dani everything she wanted to know. He ran through the scenario in his head, how he would explain to her that he was a decorated officer set up by his former partner. He could tell her about his release from prison and the vigilantes now hunting him. He could be himself. But his brain also conjured images of her reaction, which would likely involve revulsion and disgust. She would never look at him the same way again.

"You're right," he said. "There *is* a man looking for me in Homer. My ex-wife hired a private detective to track me down after I skipped town without telling her. A friend from Kentucky tipped me off just yesterday."

"You're fully divorced, right?"

"Yes."

"Then why does your ex-wife need to track you down? You're a free man now."

He was forced to think quickly and as his eyes landed on the rug in front of the fire, he came across the perfect inspiration.

"It's because of Lola. During my divorce, I agreed to share custody of the dog, but I didn't think my ex-wife took good enough care of her. When I decided to relocate, I took Lola with me, but my ex has obviously managed to track me to Homer and has sent a private detective to locate my address."

Dani was staring at him with narrowed eyes. "What's her name? You keep calling her your ex-wife but she's got to have a name."

"Her name is Rita." This was the name of his high school sweetheart, and it was the first one that popped into his head. "But why does it matter?"

"It matters because you stole her dog."

He sighed heavily, weary of the lies and recriminations. "Lola was always my dog, right from when she was a puppy. I'm her master and she only responds to my commands. It wasn't fair on her to be forced to spend time with someone who didn't exercise her enough or give her the kind of attention she needs. Rita doesn't love Lola like I do."

"Then why is she going to all this trouble and expense to get her back?"

"To punish me, I guess," he said. "Like I already explained, our divorce was very acrimonious. Rita developed a hatred toward me."

Dani studied him silently, as if assessing his integrity. He forced his eyes to meet hers and saw a mixture of swirling emotions that mirrored his own.

"You look tired," he said. "Are you okay?"

"Who is Detective Colin Nelson?" she asked, refusing to acknowledge his concern. "And why is he also looking for you? I think that his story about trying to track down a witness to a crime was bogus. He just wanted to keep his search off the record."

"Detective Colin Nelson is Rita's new partner," he said, digging his nails into his palms to distract himself from the tightness in his chest, where his heart hurt with the weight of lies. "He's helping her to track me down."

"You're telling me that a detective in Memphis is using his police powers to locate the ex-husband of his girlfriend in order to snatch a dog?"

It was the best he could come up with. "Yes."

"Why haven't you divulged this information before now?" she asked accusingly. "You've had plenty of opportunities to give me the facts. You didn't need to lie about not knowing Colin Nelson."

"I didn't know about him when you asked me the first time," he lied. "Like I told you, a friend of mine tipped me off only yesterday. I literally just found out about Colin Nelson and the private detective and Rita's plans to try and take Lola from me. I haven't had the chance to explain the situation to you."

"Where did you live in Kentucky? Can you

give me an old address so I can check things out?"

"This conversation is starting to make me feel uncomfortable," he said. "I haven't done anything wrong, so your focus on my past is unwarranted. You're overstepping."

She smiled sardonically. "That's exactly what someone with something to hide would say. And technically you *did* do something wrong. You took a dog that you're supposed to share with your ex-wife."

"I already explained my reasons for that."

Dani wasn't appeased. "Can you give me the address of your parents? Or someplace you used to work? Who are your friends? Where did you grow up? What courthouse authorized your divorce?"

She was becoming agitated, losing her composure and control.

"Stop it, Dani." He stood up, feeling the heat from the fire more intensely than before. "It's probably a good idea to end this conversation and reconnect tomorrow when you've had a chance to rest. It's been a tough day for you and your emotions are running high. You're still recovering from a serious injury and nearly getting hypothermia probably didn't help. Go get some sleep and call me in the morning. Make sure Vernon checks your house before you lock up for the night."

"Oh no you don't," she said, standing and beginning to pace the floor while shaking her head. "You'll give me the answers I need instead of fobbing me off. I can't trust a word you say, can I, Trey?"

"My name is Simon," he said. "Who exactly are you angry with here? Me or Trey?"

She clapped a hand across her mouth, clearly realizing her error. Her eyes were wide and shocked, as if finally appreciating how she'd blurred the line between him and Trey.

"I'm sorry," she said, smoothing down the fabric of her shirt. "You're right. I'm clearly very tired. I should've waited until tomorrow to come here, but I wanted to see you."

"You wanted to see me?"

"Yes. No." She was flustered. "I want to believe you, Simon. I want you to be the good, decent, honest man that I assumed you were."

"I *am* a good and decent man," he said, unable to bring himself to also describe himself as honest. "All I can give you is my word."

"We'll talk again soon," she said, heading for the door. "After I've had some rest."

"Sure. Don't forget that I'm always here if you need me. Just pick up the phone."

She stopped in the doorway and stared him

full in the face. "How can you make me feel so reassured and suspicious all at the same time?"

He smiled. "It's a knack, I guess."

"You're an enigma, Simon Walker. This conversation isn't over—not by a long way."

With that, she closed the door and he heard her footsteps fade on the porch steps. She had come so very close to uncovering his true identity. He knew he was now living on borrowed time. The net was closing and he wondered how many days or weeks would elapse until he became the pariah of the neighborhood.

Or until he had to run again.

Dani sat in her office with Jordy the next day. This was her first opportunity to speak with him since he'd searched Jade's room for clues to her whereabouts. She was sore and stiff, with a number of bruises on her body leaving her feeling like the walking wounded, but she was determined to take the next steps in the case. It didn't matter how tired she was or how badly she needed a long rest, where she could relax and forget about the pressures that were currently heaped upon her. Jade Franklin, Freddy Lomax, Simon Walker—those three names caused her sleepless nights and unrelenting worry. There would be no rest for her until these cases were resolved.

"You all right, Chief?" Jordy sat at the opposite side of the desk. "Are you sure you should be working? Nobody would blame you for taking a couple weeks' leave, you know."

She clicked her tongue at the suggestion. "I can't sit at home when there's a missing child to find and a possible killer at large in our community."

"The team is more than capable of handling the Jade Franklin and Freddy Lomax cases in your absence, and you don't have to sit at home while you're on leave. You could take a vacation. You look like you could do with one."

She couldn't deny that he was right. A vacation somewhere warm sounded wonderful. And her mom would no doubt come along too. Mia could swim and make sand castles, collect shells and run from the tide. They'd be able to sit and watch the sun dip below the horizon every night. Perhaps Lomax would even be located and arrested while she was far away from his clutches, and she could return to a normal life.

"No." She pushed the tantalizing images aside. "I may be aching from head to toe right now, but I need to be here. There's too much to do." She leaned on her desk with her forearms. "What did you turn up in Jade's bedroom? Did you take a good look at her computer?"

"Her web searches are what you'd expect to see from a twelve-year-old girl. She spends quite a lot of time on social media and You-Tube, but there's nothing concerning there. It's all pretty normal stuff."

"Any private messages or online chatting?"

"No. It looks like my Safer Schools Program might've actually had a positive effect on the kids I talk to. Jade seems to be really careful about her online activity."

"Well, that's good news," Dani said. "But it doesn't help us generate any leads."

"Although I didn't find anything on Jade's computer, I did find her journal." Jordy slid a pink notebook onto the polished desk, on which the words "Super-Secret" were written in marker pen. "It was taped to the back of a drawer in her dresser. Sonia and Nick looked surprised when I found it so I guess they didn't know it was there. It was the only item I logged and removed. There was nothing else of interest."

"That's great work, Jordy. It's exactly what I'd hoped to find."

She picked up the journal and flicked through the pages. They were filled with the type of stuff she'd expect to see in the notebook of a preteen girl. Alongside the doodles and hearts were sketches of outfits, sleepover plans and scribbled thoughts and feelings. There was a lot to trawl through and she guessed that Jordy had already examined it with an expert eye.

"What did you find out?" she asked. "What have we missed so far?"

"Jade was very unhappy at home, which we weren't aware of previously," he said. "She wrote a lot about how her parents were arguing and how she wanted to run away."

"She wrote that?" Dani was shocked. "She said she was planning on running away?"

"Not exactly," he said. "I don't think she really intended on doing it. It was just a fantasy, a way of escaping the arguments at home and living in a land of make-believe."

"Nevertheless, Jordy, we have to seriously consider that she might be a runaway. We've focused solely on the theory that she's been kidnapped, but we should consider all possibilities."

"I've planned to go talk with Jade's best friend, Tahnee," Jordy said. "I thought she might be able to give us a little more insight into Jade's state of mind."

"Didn't we talk with Tahnee already?"

"Yeah, but this time I'll be able to ask the right questions." He pointed to the pink notebook, with its childish doodles and bubble writing on the cover. "That journal is a window into Jade's innermost thoughts, and Tahnee can help me unscramble anything that she's written in words I'm not familiar with. I'm not fluent in girl-speak. Not yet anyway."

Dani smiled. "You'll learn soon enough. You're a natural with kids."

He returned the smile. "It's because I'm still a big kid myself."

"I'll get an update out to all forces across the state, letting them know that Jade could potentially be a runaway. Maybe she's been spotted hitchhiking or at homeless shelters. She's tall, and with the right clothes and makeup, people might assume she's older than she is." She stopped and sighed, her eyes growing moist. "But she's still just a little girl who needs to come home."

Jordy reached across the desk and patted her hand. "You've got a lot on your plate right now, Chief. Let me take the lead on this investigation so you can focus on tracking down Freddy Lomax. Once he's captured, you'll feel way better."

Dani wiped away the tears that she couldn't prevent falling. "I'm not so sure about that, Jordy."

He sat back in his chair, fingers laced together on his waist. "This is about Simon Walker, right?"

Jordy was, as always, incredibly astute.

"Somebody is looking for Simon and I don't know why," she said. "He told me that it's a private detective hired by his ex-wife and her new partner, who also happens to be a cop from Memphis."

"And you don't believe him?"

"No. I called the cop in Memphis this morning to check out the story but he's no longer working on the force apparently. I was told that he's taken a leave of absence. Reading between the lines, I think he's been suspended or fired. The sergeant I spoke to was real cagey."

"Sounds like he might've gotten into trouble for using his police resources to help Simon's ex-wife track him down."

"Maybe, but something's not sitting right about the story. I've started looking into all the Simon Walkers I can find in Kentucky and none of them matches our Simon. I'm wondering whether the name he uses is a fake one. What if he's living under an assumed identity?"

Jordy regarded her for a long time, seeming to carefully consider his response.

"Why would he use a false name?" he asked. "Who or what do you think he's hiding from?"

"It could be anything," she said. "He could be hiding from the cops, from criminal associates, from a bail bondsman, child support, vigilantes."

Jordy was taken aback and his brows shot up. "Wow! Chief, do you seriously think that Simon Walker is such a terrible person? I can't claim to know him well but from what I've seen and heard, he's a straight up guy. Mr. Radcliffe from the grocery store told me that one of his customers was eight bucks short on his bill and Simon stepped in and paid the difference. He also made a crib free of charge for Eleanor after somebody told him she'd had a healthy baby boy after multiple miscarriages. Eleanor says it's the most beautiful crib she's ever seen." He tilted his head questioningly. "Does that sound like a criminal or a deadbeat to you?"

Dani felt a little humbled by Jordy's revelations. She had no idea that Simon had done those things, and it certainly did paint him in a more positive light—especially since he'd never brought any of it up himself, proving that he hadn't acted to receive praise or adulation. He was obviously capable of great acts of kindness and empathy. But she still felt he was hiding something serious—and the longer he kept his secrets, the more worried she became about what they might reveal. She fell silent, now unsure of what to say.

"Vernon told me that you went to Simon's house last night," Jordy said. "And I'm guessing you didn't get the answers you were looking for, which is why you're doing all this digging into his previous life."

Dani ran her fingers through her hair and groaned, wishing she could turn back the clock. By arriving at Simon's home while exhausted, she had turned what should have been a simple procedural interview into a disaster. She should've remained calm and detached throughout but had instead been combative and irrational. Her credibility had been shot to pieces when she'd confused Simon with Trey once again. The mistake had made her seem unreasonable and overemotional, unable to move forward with her life after being betrayed by her husband. On her return home, she'd been forced to reflect on whether she distrusted Simon because of her experience with Trey or if he truly deserved suspicion. She decided on the latter. Simon was lying to her. She just knew it.

"It was a mistake to go to his house," she admitted. "I wish Vernon had stopped me, but at the time we both felt it was important to ask Simon why a stranger in Homer is so desperate to find him."

"You're talking about the guy who was on The Spit yesterday?"

"Yeah. Who is he? And what does he want? Is he really a private detective acting on behalf of Simon's wife or is there more to it? I need more information. I have so many questions that haven't been answered."

"The real question to answer here is why it matters to you so much."

That single statement was like a slap to the face, causing her to push against her desk and send her chair wheeling backward. What was Jordy implying? She wasn't emotionally invested in Simon. Not anymore. She was a cop trying to determine the facts.

"It matters to me because Simon has something to hide," she said. "And it's my job to get to the bottom of it."

"It's your job to investigate crime and uncover evidence for a potential prosecution, but what crime do you think Simon has committed? And, more to the point, where is your evidence?"

"My evidence is…" She stopped. "Let's just call it a hunch, okay? I've been around enough liars to know when somebody is being untruthful."

Jordy let out a weary sigh and brought his hands together on his lips, as if in a gesture of prayer. She knew exactly what he was thinking and waited for the inevitable rebuke. When it came, Jordy was kind and sympathetic.

"You've been burned in the worst possible way by a man whose whole life was a con," he said. "It's left you with huge trust issues and it was always going to be tough for you to get close to a man again."

"Simon and I aren't close," Dani argued. "We're just acquaintances."

Jordy shot her a wry smile. "You don't have to pretend with me, Chief. The way you talk about him speaks for itself. You like him a lot, but you need to know everything from his shoe size to his grandmother's maiden name before you'll allow him into your life."

She laughed at the insight Jordy had just displayed—and at the gentleness he'd shown by making a joke without making *her* into the joke. He was asking her to really question whether she was behaving logically, but he didn't do so by shaming her or making her feel foolish. He was a sweet person as well as a good cop, and she was glad of his considerate nature, especially at that moment, when she badly needed a friend who understood how she was feeling.

"I know almost nothing about him," she said, throwing her hands in the air. "He's so secretive, and when I ask him questions, I just know he's not giving me straight answers."

"That might be true," Jordy replied. "But it's not a crime to be secretive and you should be careful about investigating a man who's done nothing wrong."

"How do I know he's done nothing wrong when he won't be honest with me?"

Jordy shrugged. "If he's not being honest with you then there's no future relationship for you guys anyway. It might be time to walk away."

This suggestion hurt her more than she cared to admit. In spite of her best efforts to hide her pain, Jordy saw through the facade.

"Oh you *really* like him, huh?" he said.

"I guess I do," she replied, examining her nails to avoid his eye. "I tried really hard to keep my distance, but there's something that keeps drawing me back to him. I know it's a bad idea because he's a liar and I'll end up making the exact same mistake I made with Trey."

"No, you won't," Jordy said strongly. "Because Simon isn't Trey. Trey lied to you because he was a con man. Simon could be lying to you because he's scared or ashamed or worried about what you'll think if you find out the truth. You always assume the worst of people when they withhold anything because Trey *was* the worst of people. Whatever Simon is hiding might not be as bad as you think."

"How do I get him to open up?" she asked, not quite believing that she was using one of her officers as a therapist and advisor.

"I always find that the best way to connect with someone is to make yourself vulnerable."

She physically recoiled at this suggestion. She didn't like showing weakness. But she couldn't entirely discard the idea either.

"Vulnerable? How?"

"Tell him how you feel," he said. "And he might trust you enough to be honest with you in return."

"You think I should tell him that I like him even though he might reject me?"

"Yeah. If he sees you letting down your defenses, he'll probably do the same."

She laughed nervously. "I'm not sure I can do that, Jordy. I kind of like my defenses where they are."

"Sure you do." He said it like it was a no-brainer. "But they've gotta come down at some point, or you'll spend the rest of your life alone."

"Ouch," she said. "I see that you're taking the tough love approach."

"You deserve to be happy, Chief, but you'll have to take a risk to make it happen."

"Okay, I hear you." She reached forward to grip the edges of her desk and wheel her chair forward again. "Let's pretend this little conversation never happened. I'll deal with it soon enough. Show me the parts of Jade's journal which really demonstrate how she was feeling. I want to get an accurate overview of where we need to be headed in this investigation."

"Sure."

He picked up the journal from her desk and flipped through the pages. As she leaned in, she pushed Simon behind a door in her mind, slammed it shut, turned a key in the lock and tossed it away. Those defenses she'd built up nice and high weren't coming down anytime soon.

EIGHT

Dani scanned Homer Town Hall for signs of Simon, wondering whether he would show his face or whether he would avoid further contact with her. After she had angrily confronted him three days ago, she had not gotten back in touch with him, despite telling him that she would do so. This was partly out of embarrassment and partly because she had no idea what to say. She'd taken Jordy's advice and stopped researching his past. It was unethical and unprofessional to investigate a man who she had no reason to believe had committed a serious crime. Instead, she had focused on her current active cases—trying to apprehend Freddy Lomax and trying to find Jade Franklin. The latter was what the night's meeting was about.

The hall that evening was packed with two hundred or so residents from Homer, all desperate for news on the missing child and to learn of ways they might help find her. Dani had called the meeting after a request from Sonia and Nick the previous day. She had agreed that it might be a good way to galvanize local support and generate leads.

What Dani hadn't anticipated was the Franklins using the meeting as a forum to fundraise, handing out flyers advertising their crowdfunding account and asking for donations to allow them to hire a private detective. Dani felt as though she had been used, and was dejected as a result. More to the point, the Franklins' fancy private detective didn't seem to be generating any new leads. In her opinion, he was a waste of money. Sonia had reluctantly given Dani his name and number after she'd pressed her for it, but the detective wasn't cooperative when Dani had called him. He'd insisted that he didn't want or need the police's assistance and would rather work alone. He wasn't even there for the town meeting.

When the Franklins had finished passing out their flyers and making their appeal, Dani stepped forward to the microphone. "Hello, everybody," she said, standing at the podium on the stage in the large hall. "Thank you for turning out on this cold evening. I appreciate everything you're doing to keep Jade in your thoughts and prayers."

"We need more than thoughts and prayers,

Chief," The Spit trinket store owner, Adam, called from the front row. "We need results."

She smiled at him, not wanting to antagonize him or anybody else who might be sympathetic to the Franklins. Dani's own sympathies had taken a hit since reading Jade's journal. It contradicted everything Sonia and Nick had claimed about their happy, stable family and made her even more convinced that they were holding back crucial facts that could be key to the case. However, the journal's contents were strictly confidential for the time being, and Dani now needed to take great care to avoid exposing the Franklins' dysfunctional home life. Not only would it be unprofessional and unkind, but it would probably result in severe backlash from the townspeople who were determined to back the Franklins to the hilt.

"I can assure you that the Homer Police Force is committing the maximum amount of time, energy and resources to Jade's case," she said. "But we could always do with more help. That's the reason we're here, right? We need to pull together on this. We've got police forces across Alaska searching their cities and towns to track Jade down and bring her back. In the meantime, I'd love to hear your thoughts on where we could focus our searches. Does anybody have any new information to offer or ideas about what we might've missed?"

"You missed the part where Jade got abducted off the street by a stranger." This shout came from Kyle, who was sitting next to Adam on the front row. "I heard that you put out a new theory that she ran away from home. Why would you spread around something like that? It'll mean she won't get as much attention from the news stations. Nobody cares about runaways."

Dani tried to shush the crowd with outstretched arms, as did Vernon, who was standing to her right on the stage.

"Based on new evidence that has recently come to light, we're working on the *possibility* that Jade ran away, but it's just one of many theories in this case." She raised her voice above the chatter. "No matter how Jade came to be separated from us, she deserves a thorough and detailed investigation."

Kyle rose from his chair and glanced at Sonia and Nick, who were flanking the doors of the hall to welcome latecomers and hand out flyers.

"People don't want to donate money to a fundraiser to find a runaway," he shouted. "Loads of kids skip town all the time and they're seen as troublemakers. Jade isn't like that. She's a good kid who got snatched off the street."

Dani tried to fight the annoyance bubbling in her chest, but she finally found it impossible to resist.

"Just what makes you so sure that Jade was abducted?" she asked him tetchily. "Nobody knows what happened to her. She vanished with no trace left behind. Unless you're withholding information from me, you're just as clueless as the rest of us about where she went."

"I'm her uncle," he said, approaching the stage. "And I know her better than you do. Our private detective was doing great work until you ruined everything by claiming that Jade is just another no-good runaway. Our donations dropped like a stone."

"Stop putting words in my mouth." Dani felt herself losing control of the situation. "I'd never call Jade—or anyone else—a no-good runaway. I want to see her home, safe and sound, just the same as everybody else does, but I'm the one responsible for leading the investigation into her disappearance. That means I have to explore every single avenue." She repeated herself for emphasis. "Every. Single. One."

"From what I've seen, you're more interested in the carpenter who lives up on Caribou Bluff. He always seems to be by your side lately, Chief Pearce. Is your time being taken up with a romantic interest, perhaps?"

Dani groaned and leaned on the podium, bowing her head. That was a low blow from Kyle, designed to embarrass her. She didn't know why he was so hostile toward her when she had done nothing except try her best to find his niece. She assumed that all of his anger and fear was being meted out on her.

"My personal life has no bearing on my ability to do my job," she said into the microphone. "Could I ask everybody to ignore the accusations made by Kyle Mitchell? I'm not romantically linked with anybody right now, and even if I were, my priority is to serve the town as your police chief."

At that moment, Simon walked through the door at the back of the hall, took a leaflet from Sonia and quickly darted into a seat on the back row. He was pale, more unshaven than usual and appeared miserable, as if he wanted to hide away. Placing his hands on his knees, he kept his head bent, as if reading the leaflet, but she guessed his real motive was to avoid catching anybody's eye, especially hers.

"Hey, I'm not denying you've got a right to a personal life," Kyle said loudly, addressing not only her but the crowd too. "But you've been with the carpenter guy a whole lot over the last couple weeks. I'm just questioning whether your attention has wandered from Jade. Perhaps you should take some time off and refocus your mind." Kyle pointed at Vernon. "Sergeant Hall could take over for a while."

Vernon shook his head, as if thanking Kyle for the vote of confidence but declining to support the suggestion. Dani watched Simon raise his head, abruptly realizing that he was the main topic of conversation at that moment. Their eyes met and he gave her the tiniest smile and subtle nod of the head, as if to say "you got this." She took a deep breath, glad he was there but also strangely wishing he'd stayed away. He caused her stomach to feel like it was inside a washing machine during the spin cycle. She steadied her voice and tried to rebut Kyle's suggestion.

"Thank you for considering my well-being, but I won't be handing over this investigation, or any others, to Sergeant Hall." She took the microphone from its stand and walked along the stage, trying to bring herself closer to the audience and appear less closed off. "Let's get back on topic, shall we?"

"Wait up a second, Chief." Kyle jogged to the steps and ascended the stage. "Why don't we ask the folks here for a show of hands before you continue? Who would you guys like to see lead the investigation into Jade's abduction? Chief Pearce or Sergeant Hall?"

Dani had heard enough. "I will not allow you to hijack this town meeting to escalate a vendetta you seem to have started against me. If you don't retake your seat and stop disrupting these proceedings, I'll have to ask you to leave."

"What?" Kyle placed a hand across his heart as if she'd shot a bullet into his chest. "Is that how you repay my family after we took you into the restaurant and took care of you when you were attacked on The Spit a few days ago? Isn't it obvious that the whole town thinks you're doing a terrible job in searching for Jade? Somebody even wants to hurt you because of your incompetence. If that isn't proof enough you need to step down, I don't know what is."

Dani was hurt by this particularly nasty accusation and took a moment to consider a rebuttal. She glanced at Vernon, but he didn't seem to know what to say either. It was left to Simon to come to her defense. She noticed him rise and walk slowly down the center of the hall, between the two rows of chairs.

"I'd like to make it known that I have full confidence in Chief Pearce and her ability to look after the people of Homer," he called out as he walked. "She is the most dedicated, thorough and fair-minded law enforcement officer I've ever met. Who agrees with me?"

Murmurs rippled through the crowd and a few hands rose into the air, followed by a few more. By giving people permission to disagree with Kyle, Simon had created a growing opposition to his views and turned the tide on the momentum he'd tried to build.

"Why don't we give the chief a round of applause for all the hard work she does for us?" he suggested, rousing people to their feet as he began to clap. "Let's show our appreciation, huh?"

In no time, the hall was filled with the sound of clapping hands, and Dani stared at Simon in wonderment throughout the applause. Even after their bitter argument, he was still on her side. How was she going to distance herself from him when he insisted on being so protective and kind? Her feelings for him had grown tenfold even in that brief moment.

When the clapping died away, Kyle's face was thunderous.

"You're a stranger here," he shouted to Simon. "We don't really know anything about you, and you sure don't know anything about us. Why don't you sit down and mind your own business?"

"This is everybody's business," Simon replied, pointing a finger and revealing some anger of his own. "I may be new in town but I have as much right to take part in this meeting as you do. I belong in Homer whether you like it or not, and your attempt to divide these good people won't work. We're like a family here, am I right?"

The way he said these words took Dani by surprise. The pride and emotion in his voice was evident, letting everybody know that he considered himself part of Homer's family. The effect on the crowd was immediately positive. Even Adam now appeared to be siding with Simon and Dani, because he stood up and walked to the stage to look up at Kyle.

"Simon's got a point, Kyle," he said. "We should try and stay united on this, at least for the duration of the meeting. We need everybody's input and that's not gonna happen if we're fighting among ourselves."

Dani gave Adam a thumbs-up. He wasn't her biggest fan but he was doing the right thing, and she appreciated it.

"Great idea, Adam," she said. "A united front is exactly what we need right now."

She gestured toward the steps and smiled at

Kyle to encourage him to retake his seat. He bit his lip and screwed up his face like a petulant child, but apparently decided against any further arguing. He slunk back to his chair while being watched intently by Simon.

Before Simon turned to walk back to his own seat, Dani silently mouthed the words "thank you" at him. Then she made her way back to the podium and looked out across the sea of people whose help she badly needed in order to find a young girl that was relying on them to bring her home.

Simon watched Dani on the stage as she made an impassioned plea for assistance in their search for Jade. She encouraged residents to come forward with any information, no matter how trivial they thought it might be. She took questions and answered them honestly, opening up the discussion to the audience and asking for their views on how the police could do better. He was impressed by the way she conducted herself with such confidence and dignity after having her job performance called into question by Kyle Mitchell, who had left the meeting shortly after Simon shut him down.

Wearing her full uniform, Dani projected authority alongside a caring and compassion nature, demonstrating the skills required to be a perfect police officer. A twinge of sadness crept in as he remembered how he had also strived to be a similar type of officer. He still mourned his old life and always would. Only God knew why it had been snatched away from him and only God could deliver him from the pain.

Simon hadn't originally intended to go to the town meeting but had changed his mind at the last minute, making a difficult and important decision about his future after a couple of days contemplation.

He and Dani hadn't spoken a word to each other since she'd turned up at his home to confront him. He missed her. He really missed her. She'd become more than a friend, more than someone who needed help with house maintenance, more than the local police chief. He was falling in love with her, and that was why he'd decided to fight for her. He couldn't do anything about the Peterson brothers and their determination to hunt him down, but if he was going to be murdered by them, he could at least die an honest and happy man, knowing he'd done everything in his power to live a good life in a good community.

But to be the man he wanted to be, he had to open up to Dani. He wasn't sure what he would say, or exactly how much he would disclose, but the lies had to stop. Right there and then.

He'd been so preoccupied with thinking about how she'd react to his news that he didn't notice her wrap up the meeting. He was startled when she appeared at his side while the folks around him gathered their coats and purses and headed for the door.

"Hey," she said, sliding onto the empty seat next to him. "I didn't expect to see you here tonight. I thought you were avoiding me."

"I was," he admitted. "But I couldn't stand not seeing you."

"You couldn't?"

"Not at all." He twisted his body toward her. "Do you remember the last thing you said to me when you came by my house?"

She recalled it in a heartbeat. "I told you that our conversation wasn't over, not by a long way."

"I've thought about those words a lot," he said. "Because the truth is that I don't want our conversations to be over. I never want them to be over. I want to be able to talk with you all the time and discuss everything from the tiny, mundane stuff to the big, important stuff." He risked taking her hand, even though they were in public. "I really like you."

She smiled and allowed her hand to rest in his, which he took as a good sign.

"You know something?" she said. "I've been considering saying the exact same thing to you, but I'm glad you said it first."

"Brilliant minds think alike, huh?"

The hum of the hall now started to die away and the organizers began to stack the chairs, but Dani and Simon didn't move.

"Your hunch about my backstory has been right all along," he said after a few seconds' silence. "I haven't been honest with you about my life. The man looking for me isn't a private detective hired by my ex-wife. And Colin Nelson isn't her new partner."

"I guessed as much," she said with a slow nod of the head. "I tried to find some answers for myself, but Colin Nelson seems to have been suspended from the Memphis police force, so I got nowhere when I called his station."

"Suspended?" Simon was taken aback. "Are you sure?"

"I can't be totally certain," she replied. "But I've been around the block enough times to know when I'm getting evasive answers." She withdrew her hand and rested it in her lap. "What's going on, Simon? Who is Colin Nelson? Who are *you*?"

Simon looked around the hall at the remaining people who lingered around the edges chatting or helping tidy up.

"I don't want to talk about it here," he said. "I want to tell you as much as possible but in a more secluded place."

She seemed unable or unwilling to wait. Now that he had taken the first brick from the wall, she was eager to smash it all to pieces.

"Does your ex-wife know what's happening?" she asked. "Is that why you got divorced? Because you got caught up in some trouble?"

He steadied himself for what he was about to say next.

"I've never been married."

She stood up abruptly and turned in a circle, as if looking for an answer to a question that she didn't know how to phrase. Then she sat down again, her breathing rapid and shallow, clearly shocked.

"Your wife was a lie?" she asked quietly. "Rita never existed?"

"No. I made her up. Well, I used the name of my high school girlfriend—who was definitely real—but we never married."

Dani wrung her hands in her lap. "That's the second time I've been conned by a man who lied about having a wife."

This comment was like a knife to his chest.

To be compared to a bigamist, fraudster and professional liar seemed so unfair.

"The difference between me and Trey is that I never set out to hurt or betray anybody." He saw a look of cynicism fall across her face. "I only lied because my life depends on it. I'm sorry that I handled my relationship with you badly. The last thing I expected when I moved to Homer was to fall in love with the police chief. I should've been straight with you before now."

She stared at him, mouth dropped open. "What did you say?"

He tried to backtrack, realizing that he might have come on too strong.

"I mean, I have a lot of complicated feelings for you," he said awkwardly. "I'm not expecting you to reciprocate them. I just wanted to let you know where I stand and maybe we can explore the possibility of going on a date that doesn't involve me fixing your loft insulation."

She didn't smile. In fact, her face seemed to be frozen, showing no discernible emotion. What was she thinking? Was it already too late?

"You said that you lied because your life depends on it," she said in barely more than a whisper. "What do you mean? Are you in danger?"

"Yes, but I really can't talk about it here. Can we go someplace else? Somewhere quiet."

"I have to go to the station to file some new information," she said. "But I can come to your place afterward."

"You're not going anywhere alone, right?"

"No, I'm always partnered with a colleague for security nowadays." She shot a glance at Vernon, who was deep in conversation with Adam, both men holding the leaflet that displayed a smiling picture of Jade, her hair in her typical high ponytail. "Vernon is shadowing me today, so he can drop me off at your house after we're finished at the station. He won't be happy about it."

"I don't care whether Vernon is happy. I care whether *you* are happy."

She stood up as the hall helpers began to remove the chairs around them. Simon rose with her, and he stood close so there was no risk of being overheard.

"I need to know one thing," she said, holding a small section of his denim shirt at the hem, as if for comfort. "Please tell me that you didn't kill anybody."

He was sad that she felt it necessary to ask this question, but he understood why.

"I'm not a murderer. I give you my word on that."

She nodded, her expression relieved but still heavy with sorrow. She gave a little tug on his shirt hem and let go, but seemed unwilling to leave just yet. Behind her, Simon saw Sonia Franklin making her way toward them and he inwardly groaned. Her presence would definitely not be welcome at this difficult moment.

"Chief Pearce." Sonia tapped on Dani's shoulder. "Can I speak with you?"

For a moment while she still had her back to the woman, Dani closed her eyes and screwed them tight. But then, after bracing herself, Simon watched as she painted on a tight-lipped smile and turned around.

"Hello, Sonia," she said. "I'm really sorry but I have to get to the police station for some important business. Can I come by your house and speak with you tomorrow instead?"

"This won't take but a minute or two." She flicked her eyes to Simon, but seemed content for him to remain. "I know that Jordy found Jade's journal in her bedroom during his search and I wanted to know when we might get it back. He told me about some of the things she wrote inside, and I'd like to see them for myself."

"I'm not sure of time frames yet," Dani replied. "We're still in the process of analyzing it for clues, but I promise that the journal will be returned to you as soon as possible."

"I didn't even know it was there." Sonia was becoming tearful. "I had no idea that Jade was unhappy at home or that she wrote those things about running away. Thank you for not talking about it publicly and embarrassing our family. I wish I'd taken more notice of her and made more time for her." She fiddled with the collar of her blouse nervously, her skin gray except for two streaks of blush on her cheeks. "I love her very much, Chief. I'd do anything to be able to turn back the clock and do everything differently."

Dani placed a reassuring hand on Sonia's arm. "What would you do differently?"

"Well…" Sonia fell silent for a second or two as she saw Nick striding their way. "I'd stop this whole sorry mess from happening, that's for sure."

"How could you have prevented Jade from being abducted or running away?" Dani asked. "That's not in your power, right?"

Simon sensed that Dani was probing and hoping that Sonia would provide some desperately needed information. But before she could speak again, Nick was there at her side. His arm came around her shoulder to take her away.

"Let's go, honey," he said to his wife. "It's been a long evening and you must be exhausted." He smiled tersely at Dani. "Thank you for your efforts this evening and we apologize for Kyle's disruption. We're all under a lot of stress."

"Kyle shouldn't have flipped out like that," Sonia said to her husband. "He's a loose cannon."

"Let's go." Nick pulled Sonia by her sleeve. "Don't say anything you might regret later. The police will twist your words. You know that."

Simon watched Nick lead his wife slowly toward the door, their heads together, whispering. Something wasn't right in the Franklin family and their tense relationships appeared to be becoming more brittle. There was no doubt that something was being hidden.

"This town is one big cluster of secrets," Dani said, locking her unblinking eyes onto his, their pale blue color more vivid and striking than usual. "But after we meet up later, I'm hoping that the pile of secrets will shrink in size."

"Absolutely."

"I want to trust you, Simon, but my jury's still out."

She lifted her chin, changed her expression to become the police chief once again, and turned to make her way toward Vernon with a casual wave. Simon retrieved his jacket from the back of his chair—just as it was being folded up—and shrugged it on. He now had to formulate a plan of how to proceed and what to say. He couldn't disappoint Dani now that she had taken a chance on hearing him out. But he thought it might be best to impart information slowly rather than all at once, allowing her time to digest it.

The frigid night air took his breath away and he buttoned his fleece jacket, pulled out a trapper's hat from the pocket and tugged it over his red curls. When he beeped his truck to unlock it, a voice called out from across the lot, striking fear into his already burdened heart.

"Gabriel Smith, is that you?"

Simon didn't wait to meet the owner of the voice. He didn't want to deal with whoever had finally found him. Not yet. Jumping quickly into the driver's seat of his truck, he hightailed it out of there as fast as possible, catching sight of a shadow running after his truck, arm waving in an attempt to make him stop.

Before he could even consider tackling whoever had tracked him down, he had far more important business to take care of.

Dani rubbed her eyes in her dimly lit office as she clicked away on her keyboard, inputting new facts into the Jade Franklin casebook. They certainly weren't earth-shattering new revelations but they still needed to be logged while they were fresh in her mind. Claire from the Goodwill store reported receiving a donated jacket that was similar to one Jade wore. Derek from the grocery store had checked his security camera footage and realized that Jade had stopped by for candy on the morning of her disappearance. The track coach from school found a hair band in the bushes and thought it might be Jade's. These were all very tenuous leads that were almost certainly dead ends, but a good investigation overlooked nothing. Dani resolved to never stop looking for Jade and to follow up every single scrap of potential evidence.

Yet it was a struggle to keep her focus on Jade. Simon had given her a whole heap to think about too.

She already knew that he'd lied about his wife, and this made her question what else he'd been lying about. No matter how hard she tried to focus, her mind went to the darkest corners, imagining all kinds of awful things that Simon might've done. Why would he lie about his past? What was he hiding? She picked up the pace at her keyboard, rushing to finish so that she could go to Simon's house and finally put her worries to rest.

A noise caught her attention—as though someone had walked into a desk and scraped it along the floor in the quiet station.

"Hey, Verne," she called out. "Put some more lights on. You can't see where you're going in the dark."

There was no answer. Upon arrival at the station, she and Vernon had found the building locked and empty. The night patrol had been called out to a disturbance at one of the town's bars, leaving only the low lights activated, the ones kept on overnight. Dani had headed straight for her office while Vernon went to switch on the main bulbs and make coffee—but she realized now that he hadn't yet done either. That was strange.

"Verne?" she called, more tentatively this time. "You still there?"

She rose from her chair, taking her gun from its holster and peering through the glass panel on her door. The station was silent and eerie, with no trace of her sergeant.

"Vernon?" she called again, opening her office door and peeking through. Nothing.

She forced herself to think rationally. "He's in the kitchen," she said to herself, heading confidently to the small room contained within the station. "He's just making coffee."

Opening the door, she reached for the light

switch on the wall, yet the kitchen remained in darkness. That was when she realized that the main bulbs weren't working and the majority of the station was operating on emergency lighting only. As her office was on a separate circuit, she'd failed to notice. The fuse box was in the basement, which might be where Vernon had gone. He certainly wasn't hearing her calls, wherever he was.

In the main office, a figure darted out from behind a desk, crouched low and moving fast, like a scene from a horror movie. She let out an involuntary scream before quickly composing herself.

"Who's there?" she shouted. "Show yourself and I won't shoot."

Creeping her way forward, gun held out in front, she checked behind the desks, finding each space empty. The low light played tricks on her vision and she saw shadows where none existed, movement created by the passing of a car's headlights. But what she'd seen before had definitely been a person. Someone was here, hiding in the dark.

"Lomax," she called. "You don't have to do this. Let's sit down and talk it out. You did your time and you're a free man. Don't screw up your life again."

A whirring sound started up in the corner

and a desk lifted slowly off the floor, tipping sideways and sending the computer and keyboard crashing from the surface. She guessed that the desk was intended to act as a barrier, a prelude to a probable shoot-out. She rushed forward, anxious to take her attacker out before he had a chance to fire his weapon.

But when she reached the desk and aimed her gun, her mystery man was nowhere to be seen. One of the station's folded-up inflatable dinghies, normally used for sea rescues, had been placed beneath the legs of the desk and its electric pump was activated. By the time she realized that the desk had not been lifted by a person, it was too late. Giving her no time to react, her attacker moved in behind her and swept her legs out from under her, taking her down to the cold tiles with a heavy thud.

NINE

Dani was small in stature, but she was wiry and strong, usually able to contort her limbs to the best advantage. Having lost her gun in the heavy fall, she now had to rely on her fighting skills to save her. But while she could prevent him from pinning her down, she could do nothing about the hands that squeezed her throat. She clawed at his fingers, stars jumping around in her eyes due to a lack of oxygen. She bucked and flailed on the floor, feeling the rough and coarse texture of the guy's hands and arms—flaky skin that shed as she grappled with him.

Frantically feeling the space around her, she grasped at anything that might be utilized as a weapon and found a pair of scissors that had fallen from the upturned desk. Grabbing it with a fist, she swung wildly. She missed her attacker's face—covered by a ski mask—by just an inch. He let go of her neck in surprise, giving her a moment to regain her breath and swing again. This time, he was more prepared and grabbed her wrist in midair, holding fast as she gritted her teeth and pushed with all her might, as though they were playing at arm wrestling.

But she lost the game. He leaned his forehead back with one quick movement and jerked it forward onto the bridge of her nose. She yelped in pain and her eyes began to stream with tears that clouded her vision and shook her composure. Within a second or two, she had lost her grip on the scissors, and the blades were now being aimed in her direction. She had no choice other than to scramble away, her shoes squeaking on the tiled floor in her haste to escape. He grabbed at the hem of her pants and pulled her backward, but she kicked out and felt the heel of her shoe make some contact with a bony part of his body. He yelped and she was suddenly free, jumping to her feet and running to her office, where she kept a backup pistol. But she didn't make it that far. A projectile, hurled from a desk, slammed into the back of her head, sending her sprawling onto the floor once more.

She lifted her hand to her nape and felt a warm trickle of blood. Hauling herself to her knees groggily, she saw one of the station's heavy-duty staplers lying next to her, its mechanism having opened after striking her, allowing the staples to scatter like confetti.

In the next moment, he was lifting her up off her feet, carrying her like a rag doll while she lashed out with her fists.

"Stop," she yelled, trying to regain some semblance of authority. "I'm placing you under arrest. You have the right to remain silent…"

He cut her off by flinging her along the floor, throwing her like a bowling ball into a filing cabinet, where she limited the force of the impact by swiveling around and taking the blow with the back of her shoulders. As she readied herself for another onslaught, the lights overhead burst into life, flickering on with the power of what felt like a hundred suns. The effect on her attacker was instant. He clearly did not enjoy being placed under the scrutinizing power of high watt bulbs. He shielded his eyes from the sudden glare and contemplated his next move.

She took her chance. Shaking the grogginess from her head, she raced to the door, not daring to look behind or worry about how close the danger might be. Hurtling through the swing doors that led to the reception desk, she found herself colliding with Vernon, who dropped his flashlight in surprise and grabbed his gun from its holster when he saw her panicked face.

"I was in the basement," he said. "One of the fuses had tripped and needed replacing. What's happened?"

She pointed to the office.

"It's Lomax," she said, now confident she had correctly identified him. Lomax suffered from eczema, which matched the skin condition she had felt on her attacker's arms. "He's in there."

Without another word, Vernon was gone, yet he reappeared just as quickly.

"The window's open and he's hightailed it outta here," he said, holstering his weapon. "I'll make a call to the night patrol for an immediate search of the area. You sit down and take a breather, Chief."

Dani slumped in the reception chair, using a wad of tissues from a box on the desk to apply pressure to the cut on her head. Whatever conversation she'd planned to have with Simon later that evening would now have to wait until she'd gotten medical attention, trawled the town to locate Lomax and written her witness statement. She'd be busy for half the night and probably most of the following morning. Her curiosity regarding Simon's fake wife and mystery life would just have to wait.

* * *

Sitting at his kitchen table, Simon eyed the clock with concern, seeing the digital display turn to midnight. There was no doubt that Dani was not coming to his house tonight. Had she changed her mind or was there another, more sinister reason? Was she safe? Should he go check on her or would that be considered patronizing behavior toward a police chief?

He stood and paced the kitchen, hating not knowing what to do. This sensation of caring for somebody in such a strong way was alien to him. Was this how it felt to be in love? It had never happened to him before so he was flying blind. At the grand old age of forty-five, he had fallen in love for the very first time.

His cell buzzed on the table and he snatched it up. It was Dani.

"What's wrong?" he asked.

"Lomax attacked me. He somehow snuck into the station and went into the basement, where he disabled a fuse to cut the main lights and lay in wait for me. Then, when Vernon was in the basement fixing it, he attacked me. I'm okay but I won't be able to make it to your place until tomorrow."

"Are you sure you're okay?"

"Yeah, I got a small cut to the head that's been checked by a paramedic and my nose took a thump, but other than that it's just my ego that's bruised. I should've been more careful to search the station when we arrived. A patrol is looking for Lomax right now but it's probably futile. He seems to vanish as quickly as he arrives."

"How did he know you'd be at the station?" Simon asked. "He must've had inside information."

"I don't think so," she said skeptically. "Everybody at the town meeting knew that I was headed to the station to update the files on Jade's disappearance. It wasn't a secret."

"Fair enough," he conceded. "But I'd like to know why Kyle Mitchell is so familiar with your movements. He announced to the entire hall that you'd been spending a lot of time with me. How would he know this information unless he was tracking you?"

She seemed to consider this fact for a little while. "That's a good point. He *does* always seem to know where I've been and who I've seen." She clicked her tongue in annoyance. "This town can sometimes be very gossipy though. The grapevine is strong in Homer and there's always somebody watching."

"Yeah," he said, remembering the stranger who had called out his former name in the parking lot. "Don't I know it."

"It's clear that Kyle holds a grudge against me for failing to find Jade, but I don't think he's a violent man. I'm pretty sure it was Lomax who attacked me. I felt some rough skin patches on his arms while we were fighting, and Lomax has a history of eczema. The forensics team is dusting for prints right now and I'm hoping they'll come up with a match."

"I'm worried about you, Dani," he said. "I wish I could be there to help keep you safe."

"I'm not sure what skills a carpenter could bring to the table in a complex police investigation. You're better off staying home."

He'd already come clean regarding one huge secret. Revealing another didn't seem like such a big deal.

"I wasn't always a carpenter," he said. "I used to be in the force. Just like you."

She took an absolute age to reply, so long that he wondered if she'd hung up.

"You were a police officer?" she asked. "In Kentucky?"

"In Tennessee. I was a SWAT team leader specializing in firearms handling and marksmanship. I could be useful to you in devising tactics for dealing with Lomax."

Once again, she went silent. He heard only her rapid, jerky breathing on the other end of the line: a dazed reaction to his latest disclosure.

"I know this is a lot to take in," he said. "I've wanted to tell you for a long time."

He waited for a response, perhaps an angry retort or follow-up questions. Yet she remained quiet.

"Say something," he urged. "Anything. Yell at me if you like."

Click. The line went dead.

Dani had way too much on her mind and had gotten nowhere near enough sleep to cope with it all. She hadn't gotten home until 3:00 a.m., and her sleep had been restless, punctuated by vivid dreams and nightmares. In her dreams, Simon wore a police officer's uniform, but he carried tools around his waist instead of a gun holster, and when she had asked him whether he was an officer or a carpenter he'd refused to answer, leading her to wake up in a cold sweat, feeling frustrated and confused. How on earth was she going to make sense of the latest truth he'd revealed? After hanging up the phone on Simon the previous night, she'd needed several minutes to calm herself before resuming her work. She hadn't wanted to be rude by cutting Simon off so abruptly, but severing contact with him, if only for a few hours, seemed to be the only option to preserve her sanity.

"Good afternoon, Chief."

She looked up from her desk to see Jordy standing in the doorway, a cup of coffee in his hand.

"Hey, Jordy," she said. "What's up?"

He placed the cup on her desk. "Firstly, you look like you need this shot of caffeine, and secondly, Jade's friend Tahnee is here to see you. She's with her mom in reception. They say they want to talk with you privately."

Dani's interest was immediately piqued. She began to tidy the sprawling paperwork on her desk, organizing it into neat piles.

"Send them in," she said. "And thanks for the coffee."

She was still gulping the hot drink when Tahnee and her mom entered, both a little timid and hesitant. Dani beckoned them all the way inside and Tahnee's mother, Enola, closed the door behind them, before putting an arm around her daughter protectively. Dani smiled and invited them to sit on the chairs on the other side of her desk.

"I'm not scary. I promise," she said reassuringly. "Whatever you want to say to me will be treated in the strictest confidence."

Enola pushed the two chairs close together and they sat down, holding hands. Tahnee was a carbon copy of her mother, with glossy dark hair and deep brown eyes. At that moment, both sets of eyes were worried.

"Tahnee received a call on her cell this morning," Enola said. "And she thinks it was Jade."

Dani gasped. She couldn't help it. This was exactly the type of lead she'd been chasing.

"Did she speak?" she asked Tahnee, careful to maintain a smooth and calm tone to avoid spooking the girl. "What made you think it was Jade on the line?"

Tahnee glanced at her mother, who gave a smile and nod, encouraging her to speak up.

"Me and Jade have our own way of communicating," the girl said quietly. "We can talk without words."

"Without words?" Dani asked. "What do you mean?"

"Show her, honey," Enola said. "Like you showed me."

Tahnee began snapping her fingers, first slow and then fast, as if keeping to the beat of a song that only she knew.

"It's like this," she explained. "One snap means 'Yes' and two snaps means 'No.' Three snaps means 'I don't know.' There are lots of other snaps that mean other stuff too."

Enola leaned forward. "It's a very simple system of communication but you get the idea."

Dani now understood. "So Jade didn't talk on the phone? She snapped instead?"

"Yeah, and she snapped the sign for help. That's three slow snaps and three fast ones straight after, kind of like the SOS signal in Morse code. I asked her what was going on, but she just kept clicking the help sign over and over."

Dani picked up her pen and started to document the conversation. "Are you sure about this, Tahnee? Sometimes we can be really desperate for our friends to be safe, so we imagine that something really ordinary is a message from them." She flicked her eyes to Enola. "Could your phone call have connected to a bad line with some static? Static can cause crackles and clicks in your cell phone speaker."

"No." Tahnee now seemed more certain and less nervous. "It was Jade. I know it was. Nobody knows the snapping code except me and her. She called me because she couldn't talk wherever she was, and she knew she could speak to me without using actual words. I know it was Jade. She's alive and she called me."

"Okay, sweetheart, I believe you," Dani said softly. "You're her best friend and you know her better than anybody, right?"

A look of pride fell across the girl's face. "That's right. We're best friends forever."

Dani wasn't entirely convinced of the veracity of this lead. Nevertheless, the butterflies in her stomach invigorated her. What if this was a turning point in the case?

"What happened after Jade made the snapping sounds?" she asked. "How long was she on the line?"

"Only about thirty seconds," Tahnee said. "Then I heard a man's voice and the line went dead. I called her back but it just rang and rang and nobody answered."

"The cell phone is now out of service," Enola said. "We tried it lots of times this morning and the last time we called, we got a dead line. Whoever has the cell phone has deactivated it."

This made Dani sit up and take notice. All of this information was now starting to become more pertinent, especially the part about a man's voice being heard. This could be Jade's abductor.

"Do you have the cell phone number that made the call?" she asked. "We'll run a check on it."

Enola reached into her jacket pocket and pulled out a scrap of paper.

"We wrote it down for you," she said, sliding it across the desk. "I pray to God that it helps you find her, Chief Pearce. Tahnee misses her so much."

Tahnee dropped her head and wiped an eye. "I do," she whispered. "I really do."

Dani folded the paper and slotted it into her shirt pocket. "I'll get a data check carried out on this number as soon as we can. You did the right thing coming straight to me. We want to keep all our leads contained in a really close circle. Do you understand what I mean?"

"I think so," Enola said. "You want us to keep this a secret, right?"

Dani tried her best to smile in the face of a word she detested.

"You know how much I usually hate secrets," she said as Enola nodded an understanding. "But the last thing we want to do is give any potential suspects a tip-off. The person who owned this cell phone number can't see us coming."

"I get it," Enola said.

"Don't even tell Jade's parents." Dani felt that she needed to be very clear on this. "They might slip up and mention it to the wrong person. Tell nobody, okay?"

"Okay," Enola said. "We'll keep it all under wraps. I promise."

"Thank you." She winked at Tahnee. "And thank you for being such a superstar and inventing your own language. You're a really smart girl, you know that?"

Tahnee smiled, yet Dani could see the tears that were just beneath the surface. Her mother gently tugged on her hand and they rose from their seats to leave, but Tahnee seemed reluctant to follow her mom out into the busy office. She stopped at the door and turned around.

"Jade would never have run away," she said. "I know she wrote about it in her journal, but it was just pretend. Officer Jordy talked to me about her journal, and I told him Jade liked to make up stories and say stupid stuff, but she would never run away in a million years." She paused. "You believe me about that too, don't you?"

"Of course I do," Dani said with an earnest nod of the head. "I believe you, Tahnee, and you're a really good friend to Jade. She'd be proud of you right now."

Tahnee looked up at her mother and Dani saw the look of love and affection that passed between them. It was almost too much to bear, reminding her of how much she missed Mia. She saw her daughter most days but only for a couple of hours, and Mia was starting to act out her frustrations by throwing tantrums and refusing to eat. Dani needed to resume their normal routine and give Mia the stability she was craving, but that was currently impossible.

Watching Enola and Tahnee walk through

the station, hand in hand, she sent up a silent prayer for a speedy resolution to her current problem. She'd prayed so much lately and gotten nothing in return, not even a bible verse that gave comfort and reassurance. God seemed so very far away, so much so that she hadn't gone to church last Sunday. Jordy had arrived at her home to escort her but she'd invented a headache and chills, feeling unable to face the joyful clapping and singing that filled the church each week. Giving praise was difficult when she felt abandoned.

She hadn't gone to church for six months after Trey's arrest and it was only the stern intervention of her mother that had made her snap out of her sense of victimhood. She didn't want to go back to that place of anger, nor did she want to rail against God's plans. She knew she needed to submit to her situation with good grace. But, oh boy, it was hard.

"Chief Pearce." Jordy was at the door again. "You've got another visitor. You want me to send him in?"

"Sure, but before I forget, I'd like you to get a warrant to obtain the name and address of whoever is the registered owner of this cell phone number." She retrieved the paper from her shirt pocket and handed it to him. "Ask the judge to make the warrant a priority. Tahnee received a call that we think was made by Jade, so it's urgent we trace it ASAP."

Jordy took the paper and rushed from the office. Within a few seconds of his departure, another man entered, expect this one wasn't quite so welcome.

It was Simon.

"Hi," he said with an awkward wave. "Can I talk to you?"

"You look terrible," she said, noticing the bags under his eyes. His curly hair was more tousled than usual. "You slept as badly as I did, huh?"

"Worse."

"I can't promise that I'll listen to everything you have to say, Simon, but I'll try my best." She gestured for him to take a seat. "You make me feel like I'm on a roller coaster."

"I want you to know everything about me," he said, sitting down, rubbing a hand across his weary face. "So if you'll let me talk, I'll start at the beginning."

She leaned back in her chair. "The beginning is where I've always wanted to go."

True to his word, Simon began his story with his childhood in Bartlett, Memphis, growing up in a happy home with a ton of friends in the neighborhood. He talked about how he entered the police force right out of high school and was quickly recruited into SWAT due to his natural talent for operating firearms. He told Dani about the two years he spent partnered with Colin Nelson early in his career and how they became good friends. Then he progressed on to his undercover work, giving her as much detail as he could about the dangerous gang he had infiltrated and their ruthless tactics.

Finally, he reached the part about being set up and accused of murder. He opened his mouth to tell her that a police officer had been fatally shot by the gang while he was held down and forced to watch, but the words stuck in his throat. He suddenly had a terrible feeling that she wouldn't believe him and, worse than that, she would never stand to be around him again.

"You can tell me the whole story," she said, after a few moments of tense silence. "I'm still listening."

"The gang discovered my identity and framed me for a crime I didn't commit," he said. "Colin was part of the corrupt network of cops on their payroll and he sold me out."

"But the truth came out, right? You didn't get into serious hot water or anything?"

He took a deep breath. "I took a plea deal and served fifteen years in the Federal Correctional Institution in Memphis."

"You what?" She blinked quickly, her eyebrows raised high. "You went to prison?"

"Yeah. It's where I learned carpentry. I actually learned a whole bunch of other things too, like patience and humility and how to serve others even when your own life has fallen apart."

He allowed this information to sink in, giving her the time she needed to process it. She appeared to search every inch of her desk, as if reading words from a page, her face showing an expression of utter bewilderment.

"I don't understand," she said. "You were a police officer. Why did you take a plea deal if you weren't guilty?"

In order to fully explain his reasoning, he would have to tell her what he was accused of. And he just wasn't ready for that.

"It was the best option at the time," he said. "Even though the evidence against me was false, it was strong, especially because Colin gave a testimony alleging that I had confessed to him that I had a plan to start a new life in South America with my dirty money."

"But you were a SWAT team leader with a promising career ahead of you," she said. "It doesn't make sense that you would throw it all away to become a drug trafficker. Surely your superiors believed your story?"

Dani clearly had no idea of the severity of

the crime for which he was imprisoned. It simply hadn't crossed her mind that he could've served time for murder.

"Like I said, the false evidence was strong and nobody believed me."

Dani pushed herself away from her desk and stood up, still apparently dazed by the revelation. She walked to the window and looked out onto the snowy parking lot, arms crossed, head slightly bent.

"So let me get this straight," she said, her back still turned. "Your ex-partner, Colin Nelson, colluded with a criminal gang to set you up for drug offences, in order to cover up his own involvement in illegal activity. Then you went to prison and served a fifteen-year sentence. Now you're out, you've relocated to Homer to start afresh, but Detective Nelson still wants to silence you. That's why he's hired somebody to track you down. He's scared you'll try and expose him somehow, even though you're a disgraced ex-cop and nobody would believe you anyway."

Everything she'd said was true, all except the part about being set up for drug offences. It was close enough though.

"That's correct," he said. "I want to live a quiet and peaceful life here in Homer and forget about everything that's happened, but Colin refuses to let it go."

She turned around. "It's just occurred to me that your name isn't Simon Walker. That's why Nelson can't find you. He doesn't know your new name, does he?"

"Simon Walker is who I am now, but it's not who I've always been."

"Who did you used to be?"

He bit his tongue. He knew this question was bound to come, but he wasn't prepared to answer it. Once she knew his name, she'd be able to search for him online and find the gory details of his crime.

"I'd rather not disclose my previous name," he said. "Not until I'm ready."

"Are you serious? You're not even gonna tell me your name?"

"I know why it's so important to you and I'm sorry, but I want you to have some time to come to terms with the things I've already told you before we go deeper."

She shook her head, a sardonic smile on her face. "I was married to a man for three years and I never knew his name the whole time. Do you honestly think I'll allow myself to care for another man whose identity is a secret?"

He stood up to be on her level. "Simon Walker *is* my identity. My old name and my old life are long gone and Homer is where I belong now." He took a risk on adding: "With you if you'll give me the chance."

"How can I take a chance on you when you're still lying to me?"

"I'm not lying to you. I'm just omitting something that isn't an important part of my life any longer."

"Yeah, well, maybe it's an important part of my life," she said with hostility. "Please excuse me if I seem a little demanding. Knowing somebody's real name is kind of a deal breaker for me."

He took a few steps toward her. "I promise that I'll tell you in time, but I'm asking you not to rush me." The emotions bubbling inside his chest were causing him physical pain. "This is the hardest conversation I've had since I was arrested for something I didn't do. I want to make sure I don't mess up my relationship with you. It's the most precious thing to me right now." Those emotions were now causing his voice to crack. "I've never been in love before so I don't have much of a frame of reference, but I guess it feels like butterflies and longing. And that's how I feel about you all the time."

She began to tear up and turned away, presumably to hide the strength of her own feelings.

"Stop it," she said, her shoulders high and

tense. "I don't want to hear any more. I don't know how to feel about any of this. My heart tells me that I can trust you, but my head tells me to run as far away as possible. I need to be alone to think and pray and try to come to a conclusion about what path I should take."

This seemed like a sensible and practical course of action. And it was typical of Dani's character.

"I'll pray for you too," he offered. "If we both pray, then we can't go wrong."

"Ha!" She shook her head and laughed harshly. "My hotline to God seems to be out of service right now. It may take a while for my prayers to be answered."

He knew how she felt. He'd gone through exactly the same sense of abandonment and isolation in the first few months of his incarceration. Detachment from God was a terrible kind of pain—one that couldn't be filled with any other emotion or activity. In his case, the only answer was to wait for God to reveal His plan. While he waited, Simon had learned a lot about himself, about his fellow inmates and about the need for mentors in the prison. It was only in later years that he realized the endless waiting *was* the answer to his prayer. God had led him to create a prison mentorship program without Simon even understanding the divine intervention.

"When you think your hotline to God is broken, it's usually because He's standing right next to you," he said gently.

She bowed her head low, her back rising with a long and weary sigh. "It's a nice thought, but it's unlikely." Turning back around to face him, she added, "I have a lot of work to get through today, so it's best if you leave."

He nodded an agreement. He'd said all he could, and now it was up to Dani to make her decision about whether there was a future for their fledgling relationship.

"If Lomax shows up and you need me, I'll be there in a heartbeat. You know that, right?"

"Yeah, I know that. Thank you."

She walked slowly toward him, reached up to a curl of hair that had fallen across his forehead and coiled it around her index finger. Then she gently pushed it aside and snaked her finger down to his cheek. Simon held his breath the whole time, maintaining an eye contact that neither seemed to want to break. Her finger rested on the dimple in his cheek, pressing just hard enough for him to feel the tip of her fingernail.

She broke the silence first. "I wish this wasn't so complicated."

"Me too."

She stood on tiptoe, grasped his face with

both hands and guided his lips toward hers. It was a fleeting kiss, warm and soft, lasting just a second or two. It was a wonderful sensation, but he wasn't sure whether it was a goodbye kiss. He guessed that he'd just have to wait and see.

"I need some time," she said. "You can give me that, can't you?"

He smiled. "Sure. We'll talk again soon."

Leaving her office, his mind was running at a mile a minute. It was easy for Simon to promise Dani that he'd give her all the time she needed, but with a man scouring the town, calling out his old name, he wasn't sure how much time he had left.

TEN

Dani directed two of her officers toward the edge of the park where a group of parents with children had gathered. The crowd was waiting for their turn on a Ferris wheel that was lit up in varying shades of neon against the night sky.

When Sonia and Nick had been granted a license from town hall to hold a publicity and fundraising event in Homer Memorial Park, they hadn't been entirely truthful about the scale and scope of the activity. The amount of people at the event had surprised everybody, including Dani, so she had requested extra help from the police station in the neighboring town of Kenai. Crowd control procedures needed to be put into place and she required all hands on deck. The massive event certainly seemed to warrant it.

Not only were there amusement park rides

and hot dog stands, but a national news crew was filming the action, with a segment due to go live in about ten minutes. At seven o'clock, Sonia would make an impassioned plea for the safe return of Jade and for public donations toward their private investigation. CMS News had sent a three-man crew all the way from New York to cover the story, and one of their best-known reporters was in attendance, which had likely contributed to the swell in numbers. Celebrities, even small-time ones, were a rarity in Homer and this event had created a buzz for miles beyond the town.

"Wow, this is amazing, huh, Chief?" Cathy said, appearing at her side, all wrapped up in woolens. "It's like a carnival."

"Yeah, you can say that again."

Dani took a good, long look at the park, with its bandstand in the center and lawns on either side. There had been a recent thaw, and the dirty, mushy slush left behind from the last snow had been piled into the corners, where some children were now climbing up the mounds and sliding back down. Strings of lights had been draped from the railings around the park and lighted candles had been placed in small clusters on the tables set up to distribute information on how to help find Jade. Plenty of the townsfolk appeared to have signed up as volunteers, which was exactly what Dani would've expected. Homer wouldn't rest until Jade was found.

"It's a little showy, don't you think?" Dani said. "I'd expected something more somber when you consider that a child is missing."

Cathy's eye roll was clearly visible beneath the hat she'd pulled low on her forehead.

"Look at the amount of people who turned out," she replied. "I'd say the Franklins have done a great job of drumming up publicity. It's exactly what we need to get a national focus on Jade's disappearance."

Dani had to acknowledge that this event was certainly generating ample media attention. Maybe the Franklins were correct and that was the only way to keep the momentum going.

"I hope you're right, Cathy," she said. "At this point, I'm willing to try anything to find Jade. Wherever she is, she must be scared out of her mind."

"And what about you, Chief?" Cathy pushed her police beanie back on her head. "How are you holding up after Lomax's latest attack? Are you worried?"

"No," Dani denied, even though she was sure that Cathy would spot the lie. "Lomax wouldn't dare try anything in such a crowded place."

Cathy smiled in agreement but her thoughts were clearly stated without words. Lomax was on a revenge quest, which made him anything but rational. Of course he'd be willing to try something in the midst of a crowd.

"He's got some smarts though," Cathy said. "Because forensics didn't find a single print of his in the station. He knows how to avoid detection."

"He'll come unstuck at some point," Dani said, without much conviction. "Just wait and see."

"Keep in contact." Cathy held up her radio. "And put out a call if you sense any danger, okay? We got you."

"Sure. Thanks."

Dani made her way toward the news crew, where a powerful light had been placed above the bandstand to shine down on a female reporter. She was smiling and joking with Sonia and Nick Franklin prior to the filming beginning, telling them that even a hardened New Yorker like her was taken aback by the coldness of Alaska. The scene was jovial and carefree, and Dani began to wonder whether enough respect was being shown to Jade and the gravity of the situation. But maybe Cathy was right—the desired end result justified the means they took to get there.

The reporter was given one last sweep of a powder brush, a fur hat was placed on her long blond hair and a countdown to the live broadcast began. Dani watched it all unfold with a mixture of bemusement and curiosity. The news report was typically emotive, letting the viewers know about the sudden and terrifying disappearance of a local girl and subsequent police failure to locate her. Dani tried hard to keep her anger in check at the many digs at the police peppered throughout the report. Dani hadn't even been asked to provide an interview during the live broadcast, which surely would've been appropriate considering that she was leading the investigation. Instead, Sonia was now talking about her private investigator and how expensive he was to hire. She claimed he was, at that very moment, following up potential sightings of Jade across the state. She held her husband's hand while pleading with viewers to give what they could to help pay him.

Dani shook her head and turned away, immediately noticing that a black purse was sitting upright in the middle of a grassy area in the park. With nobody around it, she wondered if it had been accidentally left behind or perhaps stolen, stripped of its valuables and then dumped.

"Does anybody recognize this purse?" she

called out as she approached. "Come forward and claim it if it's yours."

She waited. Nobody held up a hand or called out in response, so she bent one knee to the ground and opened up the zipper to look for some form of ID. What she saw inside caused her to stagger backward and fall to the ground, where the wetness of the grass seeped through the seat of her pants.

Inside was a silver canister with a cell phone taped to the side. It was instantly recognizable as a homemade bomb. And to protect the public, she had to remove it immediately.

"Everybody clear the area!" she yelled, snatching the purse by the straps and racing to the edge of the park, where she vaulted the iron railings. "It's a bomb."

At the mention of this word, panic ripped through the crowd and people began to run in all directions, not certain of where the danger was located but desperate to flee from it nonetheless. Dani made it to her police cruiser on the roadside and unlocked it before yanking open the door and hurling the purse onto the passenger seat. She just managed to slam the door closed when the explosion occurred, blowing the door open and catching her off guard. The passenger window hit her on the back as she tried to turn away, and she tumbled to the sidewalk, her vision filled with flashes of yellow and orange, the hiss of the explosion resounding in her ears.

Before she could make sense of what had happened, she saw a camera looming over her, the lens focusing on her face. Without the strength to push it away, she sank to the ground and waited for help to arrive.

Simon had been watching the news at home when it happened. Right in the middle of the Franklins' interview, an explosion had interrupted the broadcast and the camera panned to a police vehicle where smoke poured from the warped and damaged doors. Dani was clearly visible, staggering on the sidewalk, before falling to her knees. The camera operator had wasted no time in racing to the roadside location to film the drama, even as Dani was disoriented and bleeding.

Now, as Simon rushed to Homer Memorial Park in his truck, he prayed that her injuries weren't serious. He had deliberately avoided the event, just as he had avoided any unnecessary public outings in the last few days, ever since the incident with the stranger in the parking lot. Only knowing that Dani was in danger had dragged him away from his home. She might need him.

When he arrived at the park, he found a scene of confusion, with the police struggling to shepherd the crowd away from the site of the explosion. Many of the people were shocked and tearful, some carrying small children in their arms or pushing strollers. Others had been separated from friends and loved ones, and they were calling out names above the throng, standing on tables to get a good vantage point. Simon tried to push against the flow and head toward an ambulance that had positioned itself in the center of the park. Dani was sitting on the back bumper of the emergency vehicle, holding her head in her hands.

"Dani," he said breathlessly, running the last few paces. "I saw what happened on TV. How are you doing?"

She looked up at him. "I took a tumble in the explosion and my cruiser is toast." She nodded to the police vehicle that was stricken on the curbside. "And the CMS News crew is following me everywhere, trying to get an interview. Honestly, I've had better days."

He smiled. Even though she was obviously frustrated with the events that had unfolded, his heart lifted with joy to see that she wasn't seriously injured and that she was her usual feisty self.

"It was a bomb, right?" he asked. "That's what the news reporter said on the broadcast."

She rose from her seated position and steered him away from the medical staff, who were assisting a handful of people looking to be suffering with shock and minor injuries.

"I found a purse on the ground that contained an IED," she said quietly.

An improvised explosive device, he thought to himself.

"It wasn't very big or very powerful," she continued. "But it was definitely designed to inflict nasty injuries. The nails that were packed inside the device would've embedded themselves into my skin if I hadn't been able to throw it into the cruiser with a second to spare." She took his gloved hand and pulled him close, dropping her voice further. "I think that Lomax is more interested in scarring me for life than killing me. He probably thinks that lifelong mutilation is a better punishment than death."

"If he waited until you were holding the bomb before detonating it, then he must've been watching."

She shivered and glanced around the park, which was now growing much quieter. "I agree. I think he watched and waited for me to pick up the purse. If I hadn't managed to get it into the vehicle quickly, I wouldn't be standing here talking to you. I'd be in surgery, having nails removed from my body."

"We have to find him and stop him, Dani," Simon said. "I almost lost you today and it was the worst feeling I've ever known."

She moistened her lips and let out a puff of white breath into the frigid air.

"I can't go any further with us, Simon," she said. "Not until you tell me your name. If you don't, we're done."

"I already decided to come clean on that," he said. "I want you to know my entire backstory and I promise to tell you everything."

"You mean there are other pieces you left out?"

"One big piece in particular," he said. "And no matter how terrified I am of giving you the full picture, I'm even more terrified of you finding out from someone else."

She held his hand a little tighter, squeezing his fingers. "I can see this is hard for you. I promise that I'll listen without judgment before I make any decisions."

"Thank you. When can we meet?"

"Tomorrow morning," she whispered. "Come to my house at around eight and I'll make us some coffee and toast. How does that sound?"

"Perfect. Do you want me to drive you home and check the house tonight?"

"No, I'm going to the station with some of the guys to write up the incident and then Vernon will give me a ride home and do the security checks."

Simon wished he could be the one to make sure she was safe. "Send me a message when you're in for the night, okay? Otherwise, I'll worry."

"Sure."

He checked the vicinity and quickly kissed the tip of her nose. "See you tomorrow."

Shoving his hands into his jacket pockets, he made his away across the grass to merge with the stragglers being moved from the park by the police. He pulled his trapper's hat low over his brows when noticing that the news crew in the bandstand had pointed their camera in his direction. The last thing he needed was to be splashed on national news before he had the opportunity to tell Dani the rest of his story.

Skirting around the crew and jumping over the railings, he decided to take the long way back to his car. It was better to be safe than sorry.

Dani winced while Cathy gingerly applied arnica cream to a bruise that was developing on her forearm, where the blow of the cruiser door had left its mark.

"Hold still," Cathy complained. "You're wriggling like a toddler."

"Trust me, a toddler would be climbing all over your shoulders by now," Dani replied with a laugh. "And rubbing this cream into your hair with a manic grin."

Cathy laughed and agreed before she finished applying a smooth layer and screwed the lid back on the jar.

"You seem upbeat, considering what just happened," she said, sitting on a chair in Dani's office. "Could it have anything to do with Simon Walker by any chance?"

Dani shot her a wry smile while buttoning her shirt cuff. "Maybe. We've got a few things to talk through tomorrow morning, but I'm hopeful there's a chance for a relationship between us."

"That's great," Cathy said with obvious joy. "I'm glad it's working out. He's a nice guy."

There was no denying Simon's niceness, that was for sure. The fact he came running to the park after seeing the explosion on television reassured her that she was his priority. And his concern for her safety getting home was touching. Trey had never made her feel this way, and she reveled in the feeling of specialness that Simon gave her. Now that he was prepared to tell her the full story of his past life, she could finally breathe easy. After all, he seemed to have already told her the bad parts. What could be worse than a police officer being framed by criminals and serving more than a decade in prison? She believed in his innocence and was even prepared to keep his history secret from the town. It was nobody else's business what had happened in his previous life. All that mattered was that he was truthful with *her*.

A shout sounded in the main office, and she looked up sharply to see Vernon running between the desks, heading for her office. All eleven officers in her department were currently on duty, assisting the forensics team in the aftermath of the explosion and reassuring the public that everything was under control. Vernon had been stationed on the front desk, ensuring that Lomax could get nowhere near Dani again, but something had clearly spooked him.

"Chief, you gotta see this," he said, tearing into the office and grabbing the television remote from her desk. "You won't believe it."

She stood up, watching and waiting curiously while he navigated to CMS News. The station was covering the Homer Memorial Park explosion on their ten o'clock show, showing the footage of terrified people running in all directions, and the smoldering police cruiser on the road. But why was Simon's picture also being shown alongside the story? She didn't have to wait too long for an answer, as the screen cut back to the news anchor in the studio.

"Former officer Gabriel Smith's whereabouts have been a mystery since he was released from prison almost a year ago. He served fifteen years of a life sentence for murdering a fellow police officer in Chattanooga before his conviction was overturned on a technicality. An eagle-eyed viewer from Memphis recognized his face during our live broadcast and called the station to report the sighting."

Dani staggered backward and fell into her chair, not quite believing what she was hearing. She, along with Vernon and Cathy, stared at the television in shock as the anchor continued.

"Smith's early release angered many in Tennessee, especially the family of the slain officer, Thomas Peterson. It's believed that Smith fled the state in order to escape his stained reputation and the public outcry for accountability. Now that he's popped up in Alaska, people will be asking why he's gotten close with the chief of police in the town of Homer."

Here, the station cut to video footage of Dani and Simon, standing close together by the medical station, his hand touching hers before Simon leaned in to kiss the tip of her nose.

"Chief Danielle Pearce of the Homer Police

Force was seen in what looks like a very intimate exchange with Smith," the anchor said, her disdain unhidden. "While his conviction was overturned, Smith still confessed to murdering a fellow officer. It begs the question why such a respected and decorated officer as Chief Pearce would risk her career for a man who killed one of their own. Only Chief Pearce knows the answer to this. We've reached out to her via the Homer Police Station but have yet to receive a response."

Dani looked up at Vernon in confusion and he shrugged apologetically.

"I'm sorry, Chief, but the messages are backed up on the front desk. I didn't realize that CMS News was trying to reach you."

"Turn off the TV," she said. "I've seen enough."

Vernon was standing by the wall where Dani had hung her certificates and awards—earned during her seventeen years on the force. She had to look away.

"Chief," Cathy said, dropping to one knee next to Dani's chair. "I'm so sorry. Is there anything I can get you? Tea, perhaps?"

Vernon let out a groan. "Tea won't fix any of this, Cathy. We've had a cop killer in the town and none of us had a clue."

"Stop it," Dani said, wishing she could crawl into a tiny space and hide away forever. "Can you both leave me alone for a while? I need some time to myself."

"What you need is a showdown with that twisted, vicious liar," Vernon said. "Simon Walker has been living among us for more than six months, fooling us all into thinking he was an honest, upstanding guy. You want me to get him on the phone for you?"

"Just leave," Dani said, too tired to even muster up any anger. "I'll contact Simon when I'm ready. I want some time to think."

Cathy grabbed at Vernon's sleeve and pulled him toward the door. "Sure thing, Chief. We'll be right outside if you need us."

The door closed with a soft click and Dani was left in silence, her previous buoyant mood having evaporated in the blink of an eye. She stared at the blank screen on the television, the picture of a younger, smiling Simon in his police uniform burned into her retinas. No emotion would come, not sadness nor rage nor humiliation. She felt nothing other than shock. He couldn't be guilty of this abhorrent crime, despite being convicted. It was impossible. She knew he wasn't capable of such evil.

Or was he?

"I didn't do it. You have to believe me."
Simon sat on an armchair, struggling to

find the words to convince her. After seeing his face pop up on the early morning news, he'd raced over to Dani's house just after sunrise, finding her red-eyed and pale in her living room, the blankets on the couch indicating that she'd slept there overnight.

"How can I believe you?" she asked, keeping her distance by standing next to the window, perching on the sill and stuffing her hands into the front pocket of a hooded sweatshirt. "You kept this terrible thing a secret, which tells me that you're ashamed of it. Why would you be ashamed of something you didn't do?"

"I'm *not* ashamed. But outside of my family, no one believed me in Tennessee, no matter how many times I said I'd been framed. Longtime friends turned against me. My own lawyer didn't believe in my innocence. I was afraid of what would happen when you found out."

She smiled a smile that unnerved him. "You had plenty of chances to tell me but you chose not to. Instead, you let me get close to you. You let me fall in love with you, and that's the cruelest part." She stood upright and turned her back on him. "After everything I've been through, you lied to me over and over. I can't even begin to process it."

He walked across the rug, every cell in his

body wanting to reach out and hold her. She'd just admitted that she'd fallen in love with him and he should be feeling unbridled joy, but there was a huge black hole where his heart should be. He'd lost the trust she'd placed in him, just hours before he was going to tell her everything. He couldn't blame her for feeling betrayed.

"It's freezing cold in here," he said, noticing the way she'd wrapped her arms around her torso. "I'll get a fire going while we talk. You look chilled to the bone."

"A warm fire won't change how cold I feel inside," she said. "Nothing can solve this problem."

"Maybe so, but all I ask is that you listen while I talk. After I'm done, if you ask me to leave, I'll go and never return. I'll always put you first, Dani, so if you don't want to see me again, I'll respect that."

She fell silent and continued to stare out the window at the morning frost on the grass. He hated that he had made things worse for her when she was already going through so much. They should be facing her problems together, not miles apart.

"Everything I told you so far is true," he said, sitting on the hearth rug and screwing up some old newspapers to lay a base for the kindling. "The only part I left out is the crime I went to prison for."

"For killing a cop," she spat. "You didn't think I'd like to know that part, huh?"

"I didn't do it."

"Yeah, so you said."

He carefully arranged the fire, bracing himself to ask the question that had been on his mind ever since he'd entered the house ten minutes ago.

"Do you believe me?" he asked, watching the flames lick the edges of the wood. "Or do you think I really murdered that police officer?"

She took what felt like an age to respond, while his chest hammered with anticipation.

"*Did* you do it?" she asked quietly, walking to his side and kneeling next to him, her feet tucked beneath her.

He looked her dead in the eye and waited a few seconds before replying.

"No, I didn't. I took an oath to protect all people at all times," he said earnestly. "I would rather have died myself than kill an innocent person, especially a serving officer. To be called a cop killer hurts me more than you can ever know, because I considered the force to be part of my family. I lost everything when I was framed for murdering Thomas Peterson and it's only my faith in God that's pulled me through. I wish I'd taken a chance on telling you about this earlier and I'm so sorry for the way you found out. I can't change how things have played out, but I want you to know that I truly do love you and I hope you believe that I'm not a killer."

A tear dropped from her eye as her face seemed to crumple, first her brows and then her mouth.

"I believe you," she whispered. "But you should've been honest with me long before now. We could've devised a strategy to keep you safe from the vigilantes. I could've helped you keep your secrets instead of fighting to uncover them. I had no idea I was putting you in danger by digging into your past."

He cupped her cheek with his hand and felt the wetness on his palm. "You did what you had to do. You knew something was off and I don't blame you for investigating me."

She put her hand on top of his and lifted it off before resting it on his knee.

"Just because I believe you doesn't mean I've forgiven you," she said. "You've placed me in an impossible position. I could be facing a suspension or demotion or worse."

"What? Why?"

"The station has been deluged with calls

since the news bulletin went out last night. Vernon sent me a message to say that the phone hasn't stopped ringing. People are demanding to know why I'm dating a..."

She stopped, so he finished her sentence for her.

"A cop killer," he said.

"Yes. Folks are pretty angry. The Franklins have already put out a blog post accusing me of caring more about a confessed murderer than Jade." Still kneeling, she pushed herself away from him, her sweatpants sliding on the polished wooden floor. "They've started a petition to have me removed from my post. They're calling my judgment into question, and there's not much I can say to defend myself. I'm the chief of police and there's video footage of me being kissed by a man who confessed to murdering a fellow officer." She shook her head. "The optics are terrible and it's unlikely that I'll be able to shake it off."

He watched her stand up and wipe the tears from her face. He remained seated on the floor, cross-legged with his head in his hands. There was no way out of this that would allow him and Dani to be together. They'd been backed into a corner, and it was now his job to stand in the line of fire.

"I'll call the mayor and tell him this was all

my fault," he said. "I'll admit that I lied to you and hid my past. I'll sign a sworn statement, go on the record and do whatever it takes. I promise that I'll make this better."

"Who's going to care about the statement of an ex-convict? You have no leverage to make this go away."

He hopped to his feet, a sudden thought coming to him. "Now that everybody in Homer knows who I am, what will they want?"

She knew the answer immediately. "They'll want to run you out of town."

"Exactly. If I agree to leave quickly and quietly, I'm sure I can make a deal to keep you out of trouble." He turned his gaze to the snowy mountains through the window, swallowing down the deep and raw pain that was building inside at the thought of leaving all of this behind. "I can be gone by the weekend and spare the mayor the embarrassment of having an infamous cop killer right on his doorstep."

"You'd do that?" she asked with an astonished expression. "I thought you loved Homer."

"I do." He had to turn away from her, not wanting her to see his lip wobbling with the effort of holding back his emotion. "But no matter how much I love Homer, I love you way more. I'm willing to take the hit to protect you and Mia. You can tell everybody that I conned you—that I lied to you and hurt you. They'll rally around and take care of you."

She closed her eyes as if reliving old memories. "It's not like they haven't had plenty of practice in rallying around me."

"You've gotta turn on me completely," he said, picturing how it would play out. "I'll go to the town hall right away and make sure the mayor understands that I'll disappear without a trace if he allows you to continue as the chief of police." He walked toward her and held her face in both hands. "You're a beautiful person, Dani, and I know you'll have a long and happy life, whatever happens."

She stifled a sob, pressing her lips tightly together and fisting her hands at her sides.

"This is goodbye, isn't it?" she whispered. "You're really leaving?"

"It's the only way."

He leaned forward and pressed his lips onto hers. She let out a muffled cry, opening her mouth and expelling a warm puff of air. He studied her face as he pulled away, taking a few seconds to scrutinize every part—the dimples on her cheeks and tiny freckles on her temples, her blue eyes and pale lashes, her small chin.

When he was sure he'd committed her face to memory, he smiled and kissed her hand before letting go and walking to the door.

"Lock up behind me, okay?" he said. "Always make sure you're safe."

"I will. Goodbye, Gabriel."

He decided not to look at her again as he walked out of her life. He'd rather spare himself that one tiny piece of extra pain. Instead, he stared at his shoes while stepping onto the porch and pulling the door firmly closed behind him.

ELEVEN

The atmosphere in the briefing room of the Homer Police Station was somber. Dani was emotionally exhausted and physically drained and had avoided mirrors all morning, not wanting to be reminded of her eye-bags and sallow skin. The telephone call she'd made to Mia a couple of hours ago had taken the last reserves of her energy, as she'd pushed down her grief and forced herself to be chatty and upbeat for the sake of her daughter. She was desperate to be reunited with Mia and fill her home with a child's giggles and chatter once more.

Dani's team of officers had been hugely supportive and sympathetic, but she knew they must be feeling the same sense of déjà vu as she did. They'd been here before—four years ago when Trey had been arrested and exposed. Her colleagues were now dishing out the same meaningless platitudes, telling her it wasn't her fault, that she couldn't possibly have known about yet another man's secret past and that she'd find someone honest and good in time. Nobody had even considered that Simon might not be guilty of the crime for which he'd served fifteen years in prison. Only Dani was certain of his innocence and she had to remain silent, forced to play along with the charade in order to save her career.

Simon's meeting with the mayor had been successful, securing her position on the force in return for Simon's quick, quiet exit out of Homer. In fact, he was leaving that very afternoon, with the official story being that he was fleeing the vigilantes who'd hunted him since his release from prison. Whatever the reason for his departure, the townsfolk were pleased to hear of it and the word had quickly spread.

"I expect you'll be happy to see the back of Simon Walker, huh, Chief?" Vernon set a cup of coffee on the table next to her. "I always knew there was something wrong about that guy."

Cathy nudged the sergeant with her elbow as she shot Dani a sympathetic look.

"I think we've focused on Mr. Walker for long enough," Cathy said. "The chief has explained the situation in full and I reckon she'd now like to move on to another topic of conversation."

Vernon, as always, was dogged in his persistence. "I know we have zero evidence to link him to Jade's disappearance but he's surely connected to it somehow. It's too much of a coincidence that a little girl vanishes right after a murderer moves into town."

Dani stood up abruptly, knocking the table and spilling her coffee over the brim. "Simon didn't have anything to do with Jade's disappearance. He has no history of child abductions, and he has a solid alibi for the time when Jade went missing. We can't pin every single crime on him just because he's an ex-con."

"He's a little more than an ex-con, boss," Vernon said, curling his lip. "He's a cop killer."

"That's enough!" Dani shouted, causing the room to fall silent, all eyes turned to her. "I know what Simon has done and I don't want to talk about it anymore."

Her officers exchanged concerned glances, uncertain of what to say in the face of her outburst. The hush that descended was mortifying.

"I'm sorry, guys," she said quietly. "It's been a really tough morning."

As she wished the ground would open up and swallow her, Jordy entered the room, his expression a stark contrast to all others—he was smiling from ear to ear.

"Please tell me you've got some good news, Jordy," she said. "Did you finally get the name and address on the cell phone number I asked you to trace?"

"Not yet, boss," he replied. "Still waiting on the phone company to release the data. I'm chasing it up today. But I got some other news that might cheer you up."

"Yes, please. I need to hear something positive."

"Freddy Lomax has been found dead in a crack house in Soldotna," he said. "I just got word that he was discovered in the early hours of this morning with a needle in his arm."

Cathy let out a whoop, threw her arms around Dani, and pulled her into a supertight hug that, try as she might, Dani simply couldn't return.

"I know I shouldn't celebrate anybody's death," Cathy said, "but this means you're free. He can't hurt you now."

Dani fought hard to paint on a smile as more cheers went up in the room, but she was numb. Lomax's death would change her life. No longer would she require a partner everywhere she went and neither would she need to activate several locks on her doors and windows to turn her house into a fortress. She could return to normal. Except normal didn't exist anymore, not since she'd met Simon. He'd opened up a part of her heart that had been wounded and scarred, almost impenetrable. Since he'd come into her life, she'd allowed herself to remember how it felt to love and be loved in return, and Simon's withdrawal from her life now was a gut punch. She didn't know if she'd ever recover from this, but one thing was for sure—she'd never forget him.

"You all right, Chief?" Vernon said, giving her a slap on the back. "You're not celebrating with the rest of us."

She shook herself out of her daydream, in which she and Simon were walking through the park, Mia between them, as carefree as any other couple. What a pointless, impossible fantasy.

"I should go," she said, rushing for the door and grabbing her jacket on the way. "I've got things to do."

"Wait up," Vernon called. "You want me to come with you?"

Weaving between the desks of the station, she pretended not to hear.

Simon loaded the last of his bags into his truck and positioned Lola on the front seat.

"Don't look at me like that," he said to her as she shot him a doleful expression. "I'm gonna miss her too."

Lola whined, nudged his hand and settled onto the seat, curling up in a ball as if anticipating the long journey. He'd booked them into a motel in Anchorage for the next three nights. Once he was there, he planned to contact a real estate agent about selling his home. He'd taken all the important and sentimental items and anything else could be removed by a house clearance firm. The thought of strangers trampling through his home, picking over the bones of his life, triggered an unexpected burst of pain. He leaned against the side of his truck, arms outstretched, breathing heavily. Leaving his beautiful cabin was hard enough but leaving Dani was much worse. For the first time in his life, he'd fallen head over heels in love with a woman who couldn't possibly be more perfect. And he was leaving her.

He figured that there was a lesson in all this pain, just like those first difficult months in prison. God must have a plan. At the moment, Simon had no idea what that plan entailed, but his faith was unshakable. Serving fifteen years behind bars would either make or break a man, and Simon had been one of the fortunate ones, because he'd served his time with his best friend by his side. God had never failed him, and it was this sense of surety that he clung to at that moment, because his whole body was full of sorrow.

He started up the truck and headed off down the track, flicking his eyes to the rearview mirror to get one last look at the place where he'd been happy and free—if only for the briefest of times. Turning onto the highway, he pressed the gas pedal a little firmer, anxious to put as much space between him and Homer as possible. There was no point lingering.

"What the…?"

He glanced over his shoulder as a dark SUV came looming as if from nowhere, racing up to his bumper in a matter of seconds. He hadn't anticipated this, too wrapped up in his own sadness. He floored the gas, willing his old truck to speed up quickly, but his engine was no match for the powerful SUV, which was already alongside him. The man in the driver's seat was signaling for him to pull over, holding up what looked like a police badge. Simon wasn't that easily fooled and continued forward, leaning across to the glove box and pulling out his gun, while Lola sat up and barked, sensing danger.

Before Simon had the chance to sit back upright, the SUV had overtaken him and come to an abrupt stop in the middle of the road. He slammed on his brake, the SUV blocking his path forward with a well-angled position. There was no way out now except to fight back, and with this in mind, he jumped from the truck while holding out his gun.

"Move out of my way!" he ordered, watching a middle-aged man in a suit exit the vehicle. "I'm not playing your games anymore."

The man held up his hands and walked slowly toward him. "I'm not here to harm you, Gabriel. My name is James Moretti and I'm an FBI agent." He pointed to the badge on a lanyard around his neck. It looked official, but there were plenty of good fakes out there. "I've been trying to locate you for a while now, but you're a tough man to track down. I got a read on your plate at the town hall and used your vehicle registration to get your address, so I've been hanging out here, waiting for you to show up on the road ever since."

"Stop right there," Simon said as the man neared him on the wet asphalt, surrounded by tall trees and the smell of damp bark. "What do you want?"

"Could you lower your gun?"

"No."

The man smiled. "I wouldn't take any chances if I were you either. Can I lower my arms?"

"Sure."

The supposed agent slowly placed his arms at his sides, the sound of Lola's barks punctuating the quietness of the air. Simon hoped that the traffic would remain nonexistent. If he truly was in danger here, he didn't want anyone else to get caught up in it.

The man began to speak. "Colin Nelson was arrested a week ago for multiple offences, including drug trafficking, money laundering, evidence tampering and witness intimidation. The Bureau has been monitoring him for a year now, along with more than fifty other officers who are involved in a huge corruption circle across the country. We're calling the investigation Operation Payback."

"What's this got to do with me?" Simon asked, his gun still raised. "I haven't seen Colin Nelson in sixteen years."

"Six months ago, we listened in on one of Nelson's phone calls where the murder of Officer Thomas Peterson was discussed. The name of the real killer was disclosed. That's when your innocence became known to us and we set about trying to find you. We're hoping you can help us build a case against Nelson and get him put behind bars for a long, long time. We arrested him a few days ago."

Simon let out a huge exhalation and lowered his gun instantly, now unsteady on his feet. Had he just heard this agent correctly? He'd been exonerated?

"Are you saying that the Bureau has sat on this information for six months?" he asked in disbelief. "Why didn't you tell my lawyer? He has my number."

"Because the investigation is still ongoing. We can't risk publicizing any information beyond those who truly need to know. And lawyers aren't always trustworthy types. We knew that you were in Homer because of the call that Nelson placed to the police chief here trying to track you down. It's been a race against time trying to locate your whereabouts before the Peterson brothers did. You're still in danger, Gabriel. The brothers don't know the truth yet."

"Once the investigation is concluded, you'll go public with my innocence though, right?" he asked, thinking how fantastic it would feel to tell Dani this amazing news. "I'll have my criminal charge—finally—fully cleared?"

"Of course. We'll start that legal procedure as soon as we can, but it's important that you come with me back to Tennessee. We can get you and your dog out on a private flight from Juneau tonight."

A million things raced through Simon's mind and his brain was unable to keep up, jumping from one thought to another as he imagined how this would play out. Unsurprisingly, the one person that was woven into his entire thought process was Dani. He had to see her.

"I've got a really important stop to make first," he said, rushing to his truck. "Follow behind and I'll lead the way."

"Let me guess," the agent called. "The pretty police chief. Am I right?"

"You got it," he said, turning the key in the ignition. "Now move outta my way because I don't want to waste another second."

Dani stopped her police cruiser outside Kyle Mitchell's house, which was located in a small clearing in the woods. Kyle had built the place himself, deliberately choosing a remote location, far away from people. Before his military accident, Kyle had been a popular and likeable man, but since being medically discharged, he'd been prone to dark moods and tempers, as evidenced by the unpleasant way he'd spoken to Dani on many occasions. She'd decided to pay him a visit today to ask the questions she'd compiled since the town hall event. Having decided to give Sonia and Nick a wide berth while their petition to remove her was still active, she needed input from someone within the family on a few potential sightings of Jade.

"Hey, Kyle!" she called, knocking on the door. "Are you home?"

Kyle's beat-up old van was out front, parked on the scrubland among the discarded kitchen appliances and piles of junk. She reckoned he was home and avoiding her. Turning the handle on the door, she discovered it was open and called into the hallway.

"Kyle, I won't take up much time. I just have a few questions. I'm not here to argue. I promise."

A crash from somewhere below made her jump and reach for her gun. Now she was spooked.

"Hello?" she called, inching her way through the cold hallway. "Is anybody home?"

Another crash sounded, followed by a girl's voice, slurred and slow, but unmistakably a child.

"Chief Pearce?"

She let out a cry of shock. "Jade?"

"I'm here. In the basement." There was the sound of a rattling chain. "It's locked."

Dani raced into the kitchen and recoiled

against the smell of rotting food and overflowing trash. The basement door was in the corner, secured with a padlock, so she aimed her gun carefully on the curved part to avoid a ricochet.

"Stand back, Jade. I'm coming in."

She popped off the lock with one well-placed bullet and kicked open the door. The basement was dark, the high windows having been covered with brown paper. Switching on the light, she descended the stairs, gasping in both horror and delight at seeing Jade come into view. The girl was tethered to a pole in the center, the chain around her ankle just long enough to allow her to reach a bed, a sink and a toilet, with a curtain to pull aside for privacy. The scene was inhumane and she could scarcely believe that this poor child had lived this way for six weeks.

She holstered her gun, ran to Jade and enveloped her in a hug, soothing her and reassuring her that everything would now be okay. Help would be coming soon. Unclipping her radio, still holding tight to the girl, she called in the emergency, asking all units to respond. Yet the airwaves were silent.

"There's no point," Jade said, her slow speech and unsteady posture indicating that she had been given some kind of sedative.

"Uncle Kyle jammed all the radio signals after I got hold of his cell phone and called Tahnee." She pulled away from Dani and looked at her inquisitively. "Did Tahnee get my message? I couldn't use words because Uncle Kyle was close but I used our special code. She understood though, right?"

"She understood and she came to tell me about it right away," Dani said, pulling out her cell and trying to make a call. "You're a smart girl—and you've got a very loyal friend."

She attempted to call the station but it proved impossible. Kyle had apparently set up a strong and effective jamming system for all signals. Dani was alone with Jade, and no help was coming.

"Let's get you out of these chains," she said, casting her eye around for a key. "And I'll put you in my car."

"Uncle Kyle keeps the key in his pocket."

A sudden fear gripped Dani as a floorboard creaked overhead. "Where is he?"

"He went to get some wood from the forest."

Dani reached for her gun and slid it from its holster, her breath shallow and ragged. She was the only means of defense for Jade and she felt the heavy weight of responsibility on her shoulders.

Jade noticed the gun. "You won't shoot him, will you?"

"I'll do whatever's necessary in order to stop him from hurting you again," Dani replied. "You're safe now."

"Uncle Kyle doesn't hurt me," Jade said. "He got mad and put a chain on my ankle after I called Tahnee but he lets me watch TV and eat ice cream most days. I want to leave and go home but he says I only have to stay hidden for another month and then I can get out."

Dani was confused. The scene that first confronted her was horrific and she had assumed the worst—that Kyle was harming his niece in unimaginable ways. Yet, on closer inspection, it was clear that Jade was clean and healthy-looking, with freshly laundered clothes and no visible injuries. None of this made sense.

"What happens in a month's time?" Dani asked. "Why is he hiding you here?"

But Jade didn't get a chance to answer as Kyle's voice boomed from the top of the basement stairs.

"You've made a huge mistake in coming here, Chief Pearce," he said. "Perhaps the biggest mistake in your career."

Dani pivoted on the balls of her feet, aiming her gun at Kyle's chest. He appeared unfazed and made his way down the stairs, an axe in his hand, sleeves rolled up on his plaid shirt, his forearms covered in some form of dried paste or adhesive.

"I wouldn't shoot if I were you, Chief," he said. "This whole house is wired to explode unless I input a code into the keypad within the next fifteen minutes. Without me, everything and everyone goes boom."

As if to emphasize his point, he brought the tips of his fingers and thumb together and splayed them wide in one quick motion. Dani knew that Kyle was capable of building an explosive device and timer but had no idea whether this was a bluff. It seemed strange to think that anyone would build a system like that…but Kyle had exhibited symptoms of paranoia and irrational behavior ever since his injury. Maybe this was further proof of how badly his injury had affected him. Unable to take the risk, she lowered her weapon.

"Why did you do this, Kyle?" she asked. "I don't understand."

Kyle raised the axe high before bringing it down sharply and embedding the blade into the wooden floor. Jade jumped in surprise or fear and backed away.

"You were meant to take a leave of absence

from your job, Dani," he said through gritted teeth. "Except you refused to go down without a fight. If you hadn't pranced around like a deer when I was aiming my rifle, I'd have been able to get the leg shot and you'd have been off work until this was all over."

"That was you? The sniper on the hillside?"

"You were only supposed to be injured," he said, as if this somehow validated his actions. "Something painful but temporary that would force you to take a break from the investigation while you recovered." He ran his hands through his hair and gripped it in exasperation. "I never meant to seriously hurt you at your house but you came at me hard and I grabbed the skillet. You're a tough opponent." He laughed. "And even that brain injury didn't keep you down, did it? You were back to being a thorn in my side within a week."

Dani studied his arms, where the dried paste was flaking. This was the roughness she'd felt on her attacker's skin at the station. It wasn't Lomax's eczema. It was some sort of residue left behind by an adhesive.

He noticed her staring and rubbed at his forearms, shedding the glue. "I've been trying to make Jade's basement a little nicer for her and it's dirty work." He had the audacity to inject pride into his voice. "I built her that bed and dresser and plumbed in a toilet and sink. And I put up some wallpaper too." He pointed. "It's a sunflower pattern. Her favorite."

Dani looked at the wall of yellow flowers and at the boy band posters tacked on top. It was a crude effort to make this dingy space homey, to turn it into a typical teenager's bedroom. She guided Jade over to the bed and sat her down, stroking her hair for reassurance. Then she walked closer to Kyle, dropping her voice, trying to protect Jade from the situation that was unfolding.

"Is the chain really necessary?" she asked. "Jade's not an animal."

Kyle rubbed at the back of his neck, shame finally showing through. "Yeah, well, she got a little bored and frustrated upstairs so she decided to steal my cell and call her best friend to come get her. We had to put in place some extra security measures after that. I still take good care of her though. We're friends, right, Jade?"

Jade looked up and smiled, giving her uncle a thumbs-up. Despite the awfulness of Kyle's actions, it looked like Jade still retained some affection for him.

"What's this all about, Kyle?" she asked.

"You wanted me off the investigation because I was close to uncovering the truth, right? After all the attacks you've put me through, I think I deserve to know the truth now."

"You'll know soon enough." He reached down to her belt and slid her gun from its holster. "I'll keep hold of this for now."

Walking up the stairs, he affected a polite tone as though she were his guest. "Please excuse me while I go make a call. Make yourself comfortable, won't you? And remember that the house is wired to blow if you try something stupid."

As he slammed the door closed, she heard bolts being slid across and his feet creak on the boards overhead. Sitting with Jade, she put her arm around the girl and racked her brains for a way to escape with her life.

"We can't locate Chief Pearce," Jordy said to Simon in the reception area of the police station. "Nobody can get through to her radio or cell."

Simon was instantly worried. Dani would never go off-grid like this. She knew better than that, especially with the attacks that had been launched against her.

"Why did she go off by herself?" he asked.

"Isn't she meant to be working in pairs since Lomax targeted her?"

"Lomax was found dead this morning," Jordy explained. "So she felt safe to return to solo duty. What we didn't realize until a few minutes ago was that he'd been dead for two weeks before his body was discovered. I just got word that the corpse was in an advanced state of decomposition. That's why we need to get hold of the chief. Lomax can't be responsible for attacking her, which means that whoever wants to harm her is still out there."

Simon turned to Agent Moretti. "We have to find her."

"I'm not sure what I can do to help," the agent replied. "If her communications devices aren't working then she's in a black hole somewhere. What were her last known movements? Maybe we can track her through those."

Simon deflected the question onto Jordy behind the desk, who was interrupted by Vernon storming into the reception area from the main office.

"What are you doing here?" he shouted, his face red and angry. "A police station is no place for a cop killer." Pointing to the door, he added, "Get out while you still have all your teeth."

Simon stepped back and placed his palms forward in a gesture of submission.

"Please, Sergeant Hall," he said. "I think Dani's in trouble somewhere. We know that Lomax isn't the guy who's been stalking her, and wherever she is, her cell and radio aren't working. She needs us to work together on this. I've got an FBI agent with me who can help out but we have to move quickly and find her fast."

Vernon flicked his eyes between Simon, Agent Moretti and Jordy, assessing whether to trust a man whom he clearly despised.

"He's right," Agent Moretti said. "If your chief is in danger, these few minutes spent stalling could be the difference between life and death."

"Dani decided to chase up some inquiries related to the Jade Franklin case," Vernon reluctantly admitted.

"Where did she go?" Simon asked. "Who did she go see?"

"I don't know," Vernon replied. "She didn't say, but she's waiting on data on a cell phone number that she hopes might crack the case. The cell provider hasn't been playing ball and she's frustrated. She might've gone to the courthouse to ask the judge to issue a warning for failing to comply with the data warrant."

"If she was at the courthouse, we'd know," Jordy said. "We can see the parking lot from here and her car isn't there."

"Give me the cell number she wants to trace," Agent Moretti said. "I have access to classified systems that you guys don't. I'll run a check on it and have the data within a few minutes."

Simon felt like shouting out with gratitude. The cell data wouldn't necessarily provide Dani's exact location, but at least they were devising a plan. It was something. He prayed hard while Moretti made some calls and Vernon shot him looks of disdain. Now was not the time to explain that he'd been exonerated. The sergeant wouldn't believe him anyway. For a little while longer, Simon was the hated cop killer of Homer, but it didn't matter. What mattered was finding the woman he loved.

"I got it." Agent Moretti held up a piece of paper on which he'd written a name and address. "The cell number has been cancelled but it was registered to a Mr. Kyle Mitchell at 791 Forest Road."

While Jordy and Vernon exchanged words of disbelief, Simon raced out into the cold afternoon.

He had to find her before it was too late.

* * *

Sonia Franklin was in tears, pacing the living room, flapping her arms and hyperventilating. She looked like she hadn't slept well in weeks.

"I told you this was a terrible idea," she said accusingly to Nick, who was standing calmly in the kitchen doorway, thumbs hooked into the belt loops on his jeans. "I can't believe I ever went along with it."

"It's a little late for regrets, sis," Kyle said from the armchair in the corner of the room, where empty beer cans and pizza boxes encircled him. "What's done is done and we need to decide what to do about Chief Pearce."

"We'll have to make sure she stays silent," Nick said. "I'm not losing everything, not after all the work we've put into the crowdfunder. Since the national news covered the story, the fund has hit the million-dollar mark. If we push hard in the next month, I reckon we might get two million. That'll not only save the business—it'll pay for the house and a new car and set us up for the future." He clicked his tongue, steadfastly refusing to look at Dani. "I'm not losing that sum of money because of Chief Pearce."

"Is that what all this has been about?" Dani

said, trying to stand from the couch before she was pushed back down by an agitated Sonia. "You organized the kidnapping of your own daughter for *money*? But you hired a private detective to find her. I even spoke to him on the phone."

Nick laughed. "Yeah, he said you were a pain in the neck, asking a bunch of questions about his bogus investigation."

"You mean he's part of this?"

"Of course he's part of this. He's expecting his cut of the proceeds once we withdraw the cash from the fund."

Dani was horrified. "I can't believe you'd do something like this. What kind of monsters are you?"

"We're decent, hardworking parents," Sonia shot back. "We're doing this for the financial security of our family. We plowed our entire life savings into The Kenai Cove to give Jade the chance of a better life. The business was supposed to be our legacy. Except..."

"Except it's failing, isn't it?" Dani said.

"It's taking a while to get off the ground," Sonia said stiffly. "Meanwhile, we're drowning in debt and the mortgage company is threatening to take our house." She glanced at her brother. "So Kyle came up with a plan."

"Oh no you don't." Kyle jumped to his feet. "This was all your plan, not mine. I just agreed to put the chief in the hospital for a while to get her off your case."

"Yeah, and you messed that up too," Sonia retorted. "Because she's right here, flapping her gums about what a terrible mother I am."

"That's hardly my fault, is it?" Kyle said, raising his voice. "She's some kind of super-woman. And Simon Walker was always getting in the way. He's like her personal bodyguard or something."

Sonia went back to pacing. "I wish I'd never started this whole thing."

Dani saw a chink in Sonia's armor and pounced on it. "It's not too late to back out. Nobody's been seriously hurt so far. If you retain a good attorney, you might not even get a custodial sentence."

"But I'll lose Jade," Sonia said. "Child welfare services will take her from me."

Dani couldn't deny this, and neither did she disagree that it was the best course of action. Sonia and Nick didn't deserve any children.

"We've never harmed Jade," Sonia said, as if reading Dani's mind. "She's being looked after here."

Dani couldn't contain her anger. "Your

daughter is chained by the ankle to a pole in a basement," she said. "You've probably harmed her more than you can ever know. You still have time to try and put right all the wrong you've done. Let me help you."

"Jade's fine," Sonia said defensively. "She's young. She'll forget about this in a few weeks' time."

"How on earth do you plan to explain her disappearance to the community?" Dani asked. "Or haven't you thought that far ahead?"

"We've got the story all worked out," Sonia said as if proud of herself for having an exit strategy. "Jade will say she was snatched by a family who forced her to be their domestic slave, until she found a way to escape and run into the woods."

"It's a stupid explanation," Kyle said with contempt. "We need something way more plausible than the domestic slave idea. We should pretend she ran away."

Dani was incredulous. "Jade is twelve," she said. "Do you seriously think you'll be able to stop her from talking about this with her friends? The truth will come out whether you like it or not. Think about it logically."

"We'll be selling and moving away as soon as we get her back home," Sonia said. "We just need to clear the debts on the house and restaurant first. Jade can make a fresh start in Anchorage, where the memories of this will fade in time. She's a good girl. She can keep a secret. And we'll have the money to give her a nice life."

"Don't forget that I want a cut of the money," Kyle interjected. "Half of it is mine."

"One *third* is yours, after we pay the private detective," Sonia said. "That's what we agreed."

"We agreed half."

As the siblings bickered about money, Nick slowly walked over to Dani and yanked her off the couch. He marched her toward the front door while she kicked and fought. She didn't intend to go anywhere quietly.

"Wait!" Sonia called. "Where are you going with the chief?"

"She can't stay here," Nick said, clearly impatient to solve this problem. "We have to get rid of her and her vehicle. Someone will come looking for her soon."

"What do you mean *get rid of her*?" Sonia asked, her face now registering a full understanding of what was about to happen. "How?"

"Well, I figure that the chief has been depressed lately, what with her first husband being a bigamist and her new boyfriend being a famous cop killer." Nick gripped her upper arms tightly as she wriggled. "She's so humiliated that she's suicidal. When the police find her dead in her car with a hose attached to the tailpipe, they'll say what a terrible tragedy it is and move on. Nobody will suspect a thing."

"No, no, no," Dani said, pleading with Sonia. "If you do this, you'll never recover. The guilt will haunt you forever."

Sonia turned her back while Nick delved into Dani's pants pocket and retrieved her car keys so he could toss them to Kyle.

"Go move her cruiser into the garage," Nick said to Kyle. "We'll do the deed in there and dump her car in the forest in the middle of the night."

Kyle rushed out the front door while Dani fought for her life, kicking and screaming, clawing at Nick and the mantel as she was dragged past it, trying to grab hold of something to slow her path. But it was fruitless. Nick's grip was too strong. She was horrified to realize that he could be right in assuming her suicide would be accepted by the community and not questioned. Her colleagues knew how upset she was to lose Simon, and even her mom might be persuaded that she was desperate and depressed. The person most likely to push for an investigation was now on his way out of Homer, never to return. Simon was her rock and support, the only man who'd know for certain that she hadn't taken her own life.

In no time, she was manhandled into her car and held firmly on the seat. Then a roll of duct tape was wound around the seat multiple times, pinning her body in an upright position and restraining her arms at her sides. As she struggled in vain to free herself, the door was slammed shut. A hose was fed into a small gap in the window, through which vile exhaust fumes were pumped, filling the car with the stench of gasoline. She knew how carbon monoxide poisoning worked. With the garage door closed, she could expect to fall unconscious in around ten minutes, with death occurring another twenty minutes after that.

She closed her eyes and prayed fiercely, deciding not to try to struggle anymore because it would lead to more labored breathing and hasten her death. Instead, she asked for help from the only source available and concentrated on staying awake as drowsiness set in. Yet sleep was beckoning her forward and the darkness was closing in.

She jerked awake as shouts and bangs rang out. She thought she must be hallucinating as the garage door was pulled up and Simon stood there, his eyes instantly locking onto hers. She watched him groggily as he barreled into Nick, knocked him to the floor and pried her car keys from his hand. The beep of the unlocking mechanism was music to her ears. The next sound she heard was the tearing of the tape that constrained her, and she was freed. Then, Dani was out of the car, being carried outside where she gulped in the cool evening air. In the background, she heard Jordy and Vernon alongside an unfamiliar voice, making arrests, reading rights and attempting to request an ambulance through the police radio.

"Go get Jade," Dani said as loudly as she could. "In the basement, chained up. Go help her. Use the landline to call for help. All airwave signals are jammed."

Jordy called out in response. "I'm on it."

As Dani sighed with relief, Simon held her close, his stubble tickling her neck.

"I'm so glad you're okay," he said. "I won't leave you again."

She wasn't sure which of them was confused.

"We talked about this already," she said, trying to clear her grogginess and focus on his face. "You can't stay. Remember?"

He smiled, and in that smile she saw a cloud

of reassurance and comfort. Something had happened to change the situation. She didn't know what, but it was good.

"I'll explain later," he said. "All you need to know at this moment is that I love you."

"You promise that you can stay with me?"

He placed her on her feet and held her upright. "I promise. My life is with you and Mia now."

"Forever?"

"Cross my heart and hope to die."

"Don't do that," she said, tracing a finger down his cheek. "We gotta grow old together."

"I never thought I'd be this happy," he said. "It's funny how life works out."

With the fresh air having rejuvenated her, Dani felt her senses return to normal, strong enough to issue a demand that she'd wanted to make for a very long time.

"Shut up and kiss me."

He laughed. "Yes, ma'am."

EPILOGUE

The newspaper cuttings and magazine articles that were strewn across the dining table covered the surface entirely and Dani was sifting through the pile, wielding her scissors to cut out the parts that she wanted to glue into a scrapbook. Meanwhile, Mia played with a dollhouse in the corner, carefully arranging a tea party in the tiny parlor.

"This piece is my favorite," Dani said, holding up a well-known ladies' magazine. "You look really handsome in that photo."

He'd taken part in so many news interviews and talk shows that he struggled to remember which was which—but this particular article stuck in his mind because the photographer had wanted him to pose shirtless. He'd refused, of course, and instead had worn his old black T-shirt. The title of the piece was "From zero to hero: the exonerated cop who won our hearts."

Dani laughed and nudged him in the ribs. "All the ladies love you."

He enveloped her in a hug. "It's a good thing that I only have eyes for you, huh?"

"That's right, Gabriel," she said, holding him close. "And don't you forget it."

He was still getting used to using to his old name again, but he always loved hearing it and reclaiming his identity had been an important step in his healing process. In the weeks after the FBI had gone public with the revelation of how he'd been framed, there had been a frenzy of press interest. He'd decided to do the interviews and talk shows in order to spread the news far and wide, ensuring that everybody everywhere would know of his innocence. While Gabriel's legal record was finally, officially, cleared of all charges, Colin Nelson was facing justice for his wrongdoing. Sentenced to thirty-five years in prison, Colin no longer posed a problem, and the Peterson brothers had dropped their vigilante campaign against Gabriel. He didn't even care that they refused to apologize for targeting him in the first place and harassing his parents. He had his life back again.

"You only married me for my tool belt," he said to Dani, tickling her ribs. "But I don't mind."

"Is that what you think?" she said, pushing him away playfully. "Well, we've been married more than three months and you haven't done a single odd job around the house. The broken spindles on the staircase won't repair themselves, you know."

"I knew we should've moved into my cabin instead of this place," he said with a fake sigh. "It was in much better shape."

"But just look at this." Dani walked to the window and gazed at the mountains, now lush and green in the warmer summer weather. "My view is better, right?"

He nestled in behind her and slid his arms around her waist. "The only view I care about is the one right here in my arms. You love this house, so I love this house too. I'll start on the staircase tomorrow."

She let her head loll back onto his chest. "The offer of a job at the police station is still open, you know. I'm sure that you're just as talented at being a cop as being a carpenter."

He took some time to weigh up a thoughtful response because in truth, he'd actually seriously considered returning to the force. Since his criminal record had been expunged, he'd been formally invited back into his old job in Memphis. He knew it would be easy to take the position and request a transfer to Alaska, but a piece of the puzzle didn't click into place. He'd come to adore working with his hands, creating beautiful things, being alone with just the Lord for company. Besides, Dani was the cop of the family and he didn't want to cramp her style. She sometimes bounced ideas off him when she hit a wall in an investigation so his old knowledge wasn't going to waste.

"I figure that I'll stick with being a carpenter," he said. "After all, it was good enough for Jesus."

"Yes, it was," she said with a laugh. "And that reminds me about Sunday's church service. We're holding a special blessing for Tahnee's parents, Enola and Stephen. Their fostering application for Jade was approved a couple weeks ago."

"That's great news. Finally, that poor girl will get some stability."

"And a foster sister who's already her best friend," Dani added. "It's the best place she could possibly be right now."

After the Franklins and Kyle were arrested, Jade had been taken into the care of child protective services, just as Sonia had feared. With their crowdfunded money confiscated, Nick, Sonia and Kyle had been unable to afford bail while awaiting a trial for kidnapping, imprisonment and fraud, and were expected to receive long sentences. Jade had been the innocent victim caught up in her parents' cruel plan, but the church and community rallied around and protected her, shielding her from the glare of media interest. Now that Jade was safely living in Tahnee's happy home, she was beginning to thrive. Nobody knew whether she could, or would, maintain a relationship with her parents in the long term, but with the town of Homer on her side, she'd be just fine, whatever happened. If there was one thing Gabriel had learned since moving to Homer, it was that the residents looked after their own.

"Maybe I could make Enola and Stephen something special to mark the occasion," he suggested. "Like a coat rack with a peg for each name so that Jade gets an official place in the family."

Dani turned around and placed two flat palms on his chest, her eyes a little moist. "That's the most beautiful idea in the world," she said. "Just when I think I've figured out how amazing you are, you ramp it up a notch."

"I'm full of surprises," he said, pleased to see her emotional reaction. "Stick around long enough and you'll see a whole bunch of them."

"Oh I'm sticking around all right," she said, sliding her arms around his neck. "All the way to the finish line."

"I'm glad to hear it." He cupped her face and kissed her lips. "I love you, Mrs. Smith. Thank you for making me a husband and father."

At the mention of the word *father*, Mia turned around and gave him a wave. The adoption wasn't fully complete but almost there, and she already called him her daddy. Mia had also met Gabriel's parents numerous times and called them Grandma and Grandpa. They doted on their new granddaughter and were in the process of selling their house in Memphis in order to move to Homer. He and Dani couldn't wait for them to live close by.

"Hey, sweetie," Gabriel said, returning Mia's wave. "You wanna help me make popcorn?"

"Yay!" The toddler jumped up and clapped her hands. "Puffy pods."

Dani looked at him quizzically. "What did she call it?"

"It's a daddy-daughter thing," he said, picking up Mia and spreading his fingers wide in a tickling hand motion to make her squeal. "We have our own language now."

"I see." Dani looked as proud as could be. "I guess you two will have to teach me."

"Sure." He put a hand around her shoulder. "We'll give you your first lesson in the kitchen."

"Can Lola help too?" Mia asked. "She likes barking when it pops."

Gabriel laughed while calling Lola to heel. "Why not? Let's get the whole family involved."

As he walked down the hallway with his wife and daughter, he glanced at the rows of hanging photographs that had been taken at each stage of his remarkable life, and he gave thanks for everything he'd experienced, both good and bad. The hardship had been worth it. He had found his way to a perfect home.

* * * * *

Dear Reader,

Having taken a short hiatus from writing, this book is the first I've written in a couple years, and I have enjoyed every minute of its creation.

The outline of the story took shape when bouncing ideas off my family around the dinner table (this is a great resource when they take it seriously), and my husband said, "What if the guy's whole life is a lie?" I was immediately hooked by this suggestion. Most people would agree that lying is wrong, especially to those we care deeply about, but what if lies were necessary to shield you from mortal danger? The tension and internal conflict that is created by this scenario makes it a perfect setup for a nail-biting romance.

Hence, Simon (aka Gabriel) and Dani came into being: two people with flaws and problems, who learn to trust in each other and in the Lord's plan for redemption.

Thank you for being one of my readers.

Blessings,
Elisabeth Rees

Get 3 FREE REWARDS!

We'll send you 2 FREE Books plus a FREE Mystery Gift.

FREE Value Over **$20**

Both the **Harlequin® Special Edition** and **Harlequin® Heartwarming™** series feature compelling novels filled with stories of love and strength where the bonds of friendship, family and community unite.

YES! Please send me 2 FREE novels from the Harlequin Special Edition or Harlequin Heartwarming series and my FREE Gift (gift is worth about $10 retail). After receiving them, if I don't wish to receive any more books, I can return the shipping statement marked "cancel." If I don't cancel, I will receive 6 brand-new Harlequin Special Edition books every month and be billed just $5.49 each in the U.S. or $6.24 each in Canada, a savings of at least 12% off the cover price, or 4 brand-new Harlequin Heartwarming Larger-Print books every month and be billed just $6.24 each in the U.S. or $6.74 each in Canada, a savings of at least 19% off the cover price. It's quite a bargain! Shipping and handling is just 50¢ per book in the U.S. and $1.25 per book in Canada.* I understand that accepting the 2 free books and gift places me under no obligation to buy anything. I can always return a shipment and cancel at any time by calling the number below. The free books and gift are mine to keep no matter what I decide.

Choose one: ☐ **Harlequin Special Edition** (235/335 BPA GRMK)   ☐ **Harlequin Heartwarming Larger-Print** (161/361 BPA GRMK)   ☐ **Or Try Both!** (235/335 & 161/361 BPA GRPZ)

Name (please print)

Address   Apt. #

City   State/Province   Zip/Postal Code

Email: Please check this box ☐ if you would like to receive newsletters and promotional emails from Harlequin Enterprises ULC and its affiliates. You can unsubscribe anytime.

Mail to the **Harlequin Reader Service:**
IN U.S.A.: P.O. Box 1341, Buffalo, NY 14240-8531
IN CANADA: P.O. Box 603, Fort Erie, Ontario L2A 5X3

Want to try 2 free books from another series! Call 1-800-873-8635 or visit www.ReaderService.com.

HSEHW23

THREAT DETECTION
Pacific Northwest K-9 Unit • by Sharon Dunn
While gathering samples on Mt. St. Helens, volcanologist Aubrey Smith is targeted and pursued by an assailant. Now Aubrey must trust the last person she ever thought she'd see again—her ex-fiancé, K-9 officer Isaac McDane. But unraveling the truth behind the attacks may be the last thing they do...

HIDDEN AMISH TARGET
Amish Country Justice • by Dana R. Lynn
When Molly Schultz witnesses a shooting, the killer is dead set on silencing her and comes looking for her in her peaceful Amish community. But widower Zeke Bender is determined to keep Molly safe, even if it puts him in the killer's crosshairs...

SAFEGUARDING THE BABY
by Jill Elizabeth Nelson
When Wyoming sheriff Rylan Pierce discovers a wounded woman with an infant in a stalled car, protecting them draws the attention of a deadly enemy. Suffering from amnesia, all the woman knows for certain is that their lives are in danger...and a murderous villain will stop at nothing to find them.

DEFENDING THE WITNESS
by Sharee Stover
As the only eyewitness to her boss's murder, Ayla DuPree is under witness protection. But when her handler is murdered, she flees—forcing US marshal Chance Tavalla and his K-9 to find her. Can Chance keep Ayla alive along enough to bring a vicious gang leader to justice?

DANGEROUS DESERT ABDUCTION
by Kellie VanHorn
Single mother Abigail Fox thinks she's found refuge from the mob when she flees to South Dakota's Badlands...until her son is kidnapped. Now she must rely on park ranger Micah Ellis for protection as they race to uncover the evidence her late husband's killers want—before it's too late.

RANCH SHOWDOWN
by Tina Wheeler
Photographer Sierra Lowery is attacked by her nephew's father, demanding she hand over evidence linking him to a deadly bombing. Given twenty-four hours to comply, she turns to ex-boyfriend Detective Cole Walker, who is sure his ranch will be a haven...only for it to become the most dangerous place imaginable.

HARLEQUIN
PLUS

Try the best multimedia subscription service for romance readers like you!

Read, Watch and Play.

Experience the easiest way to get the romance content you crave.

Start your **FREE TRIAL** at
<u>www.harlequinplus.com/freetrial</u>.